"No more kisse

"That's not what I meant and you know it.

He smiled. Deliciously wet, and wickedly handsome, he now declared, "I don't know what you're worried about. I'll always save you."

"I don't need saving."

"Don't you?" he whispered. And then he kissed Kimmie again, proving her wrong.

She certainly didn't want to be saved from this situation. After a lifetime of fearing sex because of her mother's experience at her father's hands, she felt... No, she knew with utter certainty that it would be different with Kris. She wanted this incredible night to remember forever. A feeling had lodged deep inside her that said it would heal her, pleasure her and allow her to know, however briefly, how it felt to be close to someone, to be one with them and to trust again. Closing her eyes, she rejoiced in the strength and beauty of Kris's body. Enfolded in his arms, she felt so safe. This might be an illusion that lasted only one night, but while she had it, she'd hold on tight.

Susan Stephens was a professional singer before meeting her husband on the Mediterranean island of Malta. In true Harlequin style, they met on Monday, became engaged on Friday and married three months later. Susan enjoys entertaining, travel and going to the theater. To relax she reads, cooks and plays the piano, and when she's had enough of relaxing she throws herself off mountains on skis or gallops through the countryside singing loudly.

Books by Susan Stephens

Harlequin Presents

In the Sheikh's Service
The Sicilian's Defiant Virgin
Pregnant by the Desert King

One Night With Consequences

Bound to the Tuscan Billionaire
A Night of Royal Consequences
The Sheikh's Shock Child

Secret Heirs of Billionaires

The Secret Kept from the Greek

Wedlocked!

A Diamond for Del Rio's Housekeeper

Passion in Paradise

A Scandalous Midnight in Madrid

Visit the Author Profile page
at Harlequin.com for more titles.

Susan Stephens

THE GREEK'S VIRGIN TEMPTATION

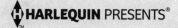
HARLEQUIN PRESENTS®

Recycling programs
for this product may
not exist in your area.

ISBN-13: 978-1-335-47861-0

The Greek's Virgin Temptation

First North American publication 2019

Printed in U.S.A.

www.Harlequin.com

THE GREEK'S VIRGIN
TEMPTATION

For Vic, a most wonderful editor,
with heartfelt thanks for all you do.

PROLOGUE

DAWN ON THE best day ever! Kimmie dragged deeply on the scent of warm blossom and ozone as she threw open the shutters of her idyllic attic room overlooking the glorious sugar-sand beach.

She could still call it off.

Ridiculous. This was her wedding day! It was far too late to change her mind. Mike, Kimmie's fiancé, was someone she'd known all her life. Much older than Kimmie and, as he'd told her himself, he'd be a steady hand on the tiller.

Or a control freak.

'Go to bed early. Stay in your bed until I call you,' he'd told her last night. 'You need your sleep. Tomorrow is an important day,' he'd added as if she didn't know.

When did I become so biddable?

Tiny bits of her had been chipped away, so small she'd barely noticed them.

Kimmie frowned as she pulled away from the window. All brides got the jitters on their wedding day, didn't they? A walk on the beach would sort her out. The sun was already warming the tiny Greek island of Kaimos, and Kimmie's bridesmaid, Janey, was only down the corridor. They could both cool their feet in the sea and, hopefully, loosen up, in Kimmie's case. But she couldn't stop the thoughts coming.

Was Mike just a safe option?

He was the only option, and she had wanted to settle on a good man before the past put a stranglehold on her and turned her hard and cynical.

Did she love him?

If love was familiarity and the reassurance of never having to explain herself, then Mike fitted the bill perfectly. No one wanted to be alone. Not really.

Did Mike love her?

Enough questions! It was time to get dressed. Pulling on shorts and a top, she padded down the corridor to knock on Janey's door.

'Janey…? Are you awake? Can I come in?'

Hearing something that might have been Janey calling out, *'Yes!'* she took a chance.

'Sorry to wake you so early, but—' Words froze in her mouth. There was no escaping the sight of Mike naked in bed, with Janey on top of him, riding him for all she was worth. Which wasn't very much, as it turned out, Kimmie reflected numbly as she stumbled backwards out of the room.

CHAPTER ONE

His FIRST DAY on Kaimos was ruined. Arriving late last night, Kris had opted to stay on his yacht. He'd thought an energetic swim in the sea would wash the cobwebs of the city away but, having reached his favourite beach, he was confronted by a group of tourists, apparently oblivious to the fact that this stretch of sand was his private preserve.

Seawater drained off his body as he stepped out of the water and impatiently raked back his hair. He was immediately drawn to a woman at the head of the group. Great breasts, fantastic legs and the most eye-catching waist-length ebony hair streaked with purple. Wearing the tiniest bikini he'd ever seen, she was dancing down the dunes to the sound of an old beatbox one of her companions was carrying on his shoulder. She'd tied a brightly coloured chiffon scarf around her waist and it was decorated with something that flashed in the sun. Tiny bells attached to it jingled as she moved. There were so many strings of beads around her neck that if she went in the water, she'd surely sink. He liked quirky, but this was ridiculous, though her manner interested him as much as her looks. There was something wild, almost reckless in her behaviour, as if she had nothing to lose and was dancing to blot out some unpleasant incident. No doubt in on the facts, he guessed her friends were trying to show their support.

What the hell? His hackles rose as they started to light a bonfire. *On his beach!* Then someone produced a dress from a sack—it looked like a wedding gown. Did it belong to the quirky woman? Yes, he gathered as she refused to touch it and, pulling a face, stepped back, leaving her friends to place it on the funeral pyre.

Resentment clawed at his gut, but he was keen to see the drama play out. As the flames rose and the dress disintegrated, the woman remained motionless, watching. Her friends, having formed a protective circle around her, also remained still until the fire had guttered and gone out. With only ashes left, she stabbed at the embers with a stick, as if she had to be sure that every atom of the gown had been completely consumed. Dropping the stick, she walked to the water's edge where, tugging a ring off her finger, she flung it into the sea. He watched it glint as it went out and glint again as a strong wave brought it straight back onto the beach again. The tide was working against her, though she had no idea that the ring had returned as she'd already turned away.

Wanting to meet her for some reason he didn't examine too closely, he retrieved the ring and caught up with her before she reached her friends. Holding it out on the palm of his hand, he asked, 'Is this yours?'

She stared at him in silence for a moment, and then her gaze dropped to his outstretched hand and she shuddered.

'Take it, or I can toss it back,' he offered.

Kimmie was in turmoil. Her heart was jumping in her chest. Not only had she survived the shock of her life this morning, and then tried to make things good for her friends, she was now confronted by a Titan who might have stepped straight out of myth and legend. And he was holding out the ring, expecting her to take it.

She guessed he was around thirty years old. Huge and brutally masculine, he was the last thing she needed today. A piercingly intelligent stare that wouldn't let her go, and hard, rugged features that looked as if they'd been hewn out of stone completed a picture she had no wish to see. His wild mop of thick, inky-black hair was still damp from the sea, and had caught on his sharply etched cheekbones thanks to the thick shading of black stubble that suggested he hadn't shaved today. Tough enough to be a roustabout from the docks, she guessed he might be a local fisherman. Deeply bronzed by the elements, his body could have been sculpted by Michelangelo.

'You found it,' she said lamely, finding her voice.

'Evidently,' he confirmed.

'But I don't understand.' She frowned. 'I just flung it out to sea.'

'And the tide brought it straight back again. I thought you'd want to know,' he remarked in perfect English. His voice was deep and husky, and only faintly accented—Greek, she thought, having recognised the familiar intonation. So he was a well-travelled roustabout.

'Yes, thank you,' she said, shading her eyes to stare up at him.

'And now you'd like me to throw it back again,' he guessed with an amused quirk of his brow.

'Would you?'

'Of course.'

'Can you make sure it doesn't come back again?'

'It won't ever come back,' he assured her, glancing at her hand on his arm.

What was she thinking?

She wasn't thinking, Kimmie concluded as she snatched her hand away from his arm. Shock had sent her reeling this morning, and stunned amazement at seeing this man had halted her recovery stone dead.

But he was as good as his word. She watched as he fired the ring so far out to sea she was confident it would never be seen again. Her gaze strayed to the formidable width of his shoulders. He was as stunning from the back as he was from his front.

'So something went wrong for you today,' he said as he swung around.

She almost jumped out of her skin, embarrassed to think he might have caught her staring at him. 'You could say that,' she admitted sparingly.

'Everyone has bad days.' His magnificent shoulders eased in a shrug.

'This one was extremely bad,' she admitted.

'Yet it prompted a party?' he queried.

'It's more of a wake,' she explained, turning to glance at her friends, who were already dancing on the flat, damp sand at the edge of the beach. They seemed to be having a good time, which was all she wanted.

'A wake?' the Titan prompted.

'I don't want to answer any more questions,' she said bluntly. Walking into Janey's room that morning had been quite enough. Staring into the mirror later, and realising she could never compete with Janey's polish, wasn't something she wanted to relive either.

'Fair enough. Glad to be of service,' the Titan drawled.

As she filled her eyes with him, her mind raced to work out how she'd reached this point. She'd been a scholarship girl, which was how she'd first met Mike's sister. Jocelyn had taken Kimmie home for the holidays, which was where she'd met Mike. It was no wonder suave, sophisticated Mike had ultimately grown bored with Kimmie and looked elsewhere. She just wished he'd done that before asking her to marry him.

'Don't let me keep you,' she said to the Titan.

One satanic brow lifted and she guessed he didn't make a habit of doing other people's bidding. And that posed another question. Why had he approached her now? Why Kimmie? She couldn't bear it if he felt sorry for her…if anyone felt sorry for her. She'd sort this out herself.

Lifting her chin, she said, 'Can I offer you a drink to say thank you?' In her peripheral vision she could see her friends setting out the picnic they'd brought with them. Their landlady, Kyria Demetriou, had prepared the most wonderful wedding breakfast, and Kimmie was determined it wouldn't go to waste.

'I appreciate your offer,' he said, 'but I won't be able to accept as you and your friends must leave.'

'I'm sorry?' She gazed up, uncomprehending.

'This is a private beach,' he explained, 'and you don't have the necessary permission to be here.'

'And you do?' she challenged. It might have been a hell of a day, but she wasn't on the canvas yet, and she had no intention of going down without a fight. Her guests had travelled a long way, only to have the wedding cancelled at the eleventh hour. The least she could offer them was a party on the beach.

'Look,' she reasoned when the man remained stony-faced, 'we're not doing any harm, and we'll clear everything up when we leave.'

'Read the notice,' he rapped.

She followed his stare to a huge red sign proclaiming the beach off-limits to the general public.

'I'm sorry. I didn't see it,' she admitted. 'Are you some sort of ranger?' Her heart thumped wildly as she stared him up and down.

'Let's just say I'm an interested party.'

'Perhaps you can show me a letter of authority?' She realised how foolish that request was even as she said it. More proof, if she had needed it, that she was only firing on half-cylinders.

The man seemed to find this amusing and flicked a glance down his half-naked frame. 'I'm afraid I don't have anything on me at the moment.'

She refused to look at his bronzed perfection, and wasn't in the mood to back down. 'With no proof of your authority, we're not going anywhere.'

The temperature rose between them. 'Just pack up this circus and leave.'

'Is that the type of welcome you'd like me to associate with Kaimos?'

'You'll have plenty to remember,' he flashed back.

'How nice of you to remind me.'

His expression remained unchanged.

'It would be nice to have some good memories to mix in with the bad, but if you can't help me...' She shrugged. 'Can't I say anything to change your mind?'

The man remained silent.

'Are you a member of the crew from that mega-yacht out there?' she asked, trying another tack. 'Did you swim to the beach from that...?' She could only be pleasant for so long under this sort of pressure. 'That floating office block?' The huge vessel had been moored up in the bay since first thing that morning. It was the type of eye-popping craft favoured by billionaires and potentates. If he worked for someone like that, she could understand that he'd want to clear the beach before his boss came on shore.

'Crew?' he queried, frowning. 'Floating office block?'

'That boat out there,' she said, pointing.

If only her pulse would slow down and her wits would speed up, she thought as he replied in a clipped tone, 'I'm not crew. And the vessel you refer to is the *Spirit of Kaimos*.'

'Well, I'm very sorry, but I've never heard of it. And you still haven't answered my question. Where are you from?'

'Why is that so important?'

'It isn't. I'm just curious.'

'As am I,' he shot back.

His lazy gaze stripped her bare and, while her wilful body applauded, her mind sensibly screamed, *This isn't right... I need recovery time... What am I doing here, trading insults with a sexy stranger?*

All Kimmie had wanted when she came to the seashore was to dance all the bad stuff out of her head. Instead she was getting deeper into conflict with a man who thought he could order her friends off the beach. She'd reached her tipping point. It was enough to know she'd let everyone down by bringing them all the way to Greece for a wedding that wasn't going to happen, without having some arrogant Titan order them to leave.

'Talk and I might let you stay.'

Kimmie's jaw firmed and her eyes flashed fire at him, but she had her friends to consider. Curbing her anger threw her thoughts back to the mistakes of the day. She should have seen that Mike's romantic interest in her had only grown wings when her exhibition of paintings straight out of college had been such an unexpected success. That should have rung warning bells, but Jocelyn was like a sister and Kimmie loved her dearly, and she had so wanted to belong and have a family of her own. Mike couldn't wait to share everything with her, he'd said. Now she realised the only thing he'd actually meant to share with her was the money she'd made from the sale of her paintings. And now this man wanted to take another bite out of her life?

'I'm not here to sort out your problems,' he rapped, confirming her impression of him as harsh and unfeeling. 'Or to be the butt of your anger,' he added in the same hostile tone.

She stared him straight in the eyes. He might terrify some people, but she'd been through the wringer today and had no intention of backing down, though she had to handle him carefully for the sake of her friends.

'Without proof that you have the authority to tell us to leave, I don't see why we should.'

'I'm asking you politely to leave,' he emphasised.

'And I'm telling you equally politely that we're not doing any harm, and that we'll leave the beach exactly as we found it.'

She was wholly in the wrong, but she'd impressed him. Determined to defy him, after what could only have been one hell of a start to her day, he guessed what she'd really like to do was to find a dark, quiet place where she could be alone with her thoughts as she tried to work out what had gone wrong. She struck him as an intelligent woman, not the type to blunder into a hasty marriage, so he was curious too. To her credit, she was concentrating on her friends, doing everything she could to make things right for them. This included holding him at bay, which was no mean task. He was used to women waiting for him to call the shots before falling in line with whatever he wanted. This woman would never do that. He found himself in the unusual position of telling her to go while wanting her to stay. In the interest of compromise he decided to back off for a while.

'Kris,' he said, extending his hand in the customary greeting.

Ignoring his hand, she frowned suspiciously. 'Does that mean you're joining us?'

'I didn't say that.' He noted the flush in her cheeks and her darkening eyes as his hand closed around hers. The urge to drag her close and kiss her hard was overwhelming, but control was second nature to him.

Displaying the same iron resolve, she stepped back, pulling her hand out of his. 'Kimmie—Kimmie Lancaster. Kimmie isn't short for anything; it's just Kimmie.'

This woman wasn't *just* anything. 'So, *just* Kimmie…burning a wedding dress and throwing away a diamond ring, and now you're having a party.'

'A wedding wake,' she reminded him. 'We can't waste the food. Kyria Demetriou at the Oia Mare, where we're staying, went to so much trouble to prepare a wedding feast, and this is the only way we can show our appreciation.'

'Commendable. She's a friend of mine.'

'Kyria Demetriou?'

'Yes.'

Kyria Demetriou was a pretty good judge of character, and he could see Kimmie thinking, *Okay, so maybe he's not so bad.*

'It's a small island,' she said. 'I'm not surprised you know each other. I don't expect you'd want us saying anything bad about you to her?'

'Are you attempting to blackmail me?' he asked, smiling faintly with incredulity.

'Whatever it takes,' she said bluntly.

More gripped by her character than ever, he pressed on with his low-key interrogation. 'The Oia Mare is very nice, but quite expensive…?'

'I wanted to treat my friends—'

'*You* wanted to treat your friends?'

'What's wrong with that?' she fired back.

'It must have cost you a lot of money.'

She didn't answer.

'Why couldn't your friends contribute towards the cost themselves?' he prompted.

'Because I didn't want them to. I'd had a lucky break and wanted to share my good fortune. I ring-fenced some of the money I'd made for a project I'm interested in, but there was plenty left over and I wanted us all to do something special, something different for a change.'

'And your fiancé went along with this proposal?'

She clammed up, and then admitted, 'I don't even know why I'm telling you all this.'

'Because you need to get it off your chest?'

Pressing her lips down, she shrugged.

'Were you engaged for long?'

He could see her wondering whether to say another word, but then her armour cracked and she revealed, 'If I tell you, you'll laugh.'

'Try me,' he challenged.

'All right, I will. I'm an artist, recently graduated from studying at college in London. My first art exhibition was held straight out of college. No one, least of all me, could have predicted what a success it would be. My *ex*-fiancé is an older man whom I've known pretty much all my life. He's my best friend's older brother. Anyway,' she added, brushing off unpleasant memories, he guessed, 'he came to the gallery on the last night when there was nothing left to buy. I think we were both amazed…buoyed up… excited by what had happened. And he proposed to me there and then.'

'And you agreed to marry him there and then?'

'Yes. It does sound stupid now,' she agreed wearily, 'but sometimes life pushes you down a path you don't expect, because the past is steering you.'

'Is that what happened in your case?'

She looked at him for a few long moments and then said, 'I'm done. I'm not going to tell you anything else.'

'Quite right,' he agreed reluctantly.

Life choices. And where had they got her? Kimmie huffed inwardly as she realised that in the personal sense her choices had been disastrous. She'd jumped at the chance to marry Mike, thinking she would be laughing in the face of the past. She could see now he'd caught her at the very best…no, the very worst possible moment.

'So your fiancé cheated on you?' Kris guessed shrewdly.

'What brilliant powers of deduction.'

'A bride without a groom,' he added, unfazed by her sarcasm. 'How unfortunate.'

'Some would call it lucky.'

'Do you?' he asked with a keen stare.

'I call it a life lesson,' she admitted.

'Will it make you bitter?'

'No,' she said without hesitation. 'It will make me cautious, and determined never to make the same mistake again.'

'Easy to say, harder to do,' Kris observed.

'You don't know me,' she assured him.

'That sounds like a challenge,' he said lazily.

An idea had begun to brew in Kris's mind. He'd have to explore the possibility a lot more before deciding to progress things further, but this unexpected encounter, coming hot on the heels of a conversation he'd had with his uncle, made him feel as if fate was lending a hand.

'Well, if you're not going to join us, I guess I'll see you around,' she said pointedly.

'It will be hard to avoid you on such a small island.'

'I'll do my best to stay out of your way.'

'Starting now?' he suggested, shooting a mean-ingful glance at her friends.

She sighed. 'Not that again. I promise we'll be ultra-careful. I'll be personally responsible for mak-ing sure that every grain of sand is returned to its rightful place before we leave.'

He huffed a laugh. She'd won. Whether that was because she was so unusual, or because she'd stood up to him, he didn't know and didn't care.

'Make sure you do that,' he warned lightly. 'Or you'll answer to me.'

The blush on her face suggested that wasn't an entirely unwelcome proposition. She was extremely attractive, like no one he'd ever met before. He liked a challenge and he admired her grit. With their stares locked in mutual interest, he wondered if her body ached like his. Animals would have cut to the chase by now, but humans were bound by rules of conven-tion. Getting to know her would take time.

'Why don't you introduce me around?' he sug-gested.

CHAPTER TWO

WHAT WAS SHE getting herself into now? Kimmie wondered as she introduced Kris to her friends. Was her brain so fried after finding two people she had trusted in bed together that she was more than capable of acting out of character to the point of being reckless? There was a sense of unreality about things, of not quite touching base with events that seemed to be floating over her head. Frying pan and fire came to mind. She stared at Kris, who was behaving quite differently to the autocratic tyrant he'd initially seemed on the beach. What had changed him? Why was he being so charming? Did Kris have an angle too?

'He's really nice,' one of her friends said.

'*Look what I found on the beach* is a great opener when the flotsam looks like Kris,' Kimmie admitted.

She'd tried the conventional kind of relationship and look how that had turned out, Kimmie mused as Kris continued to talk easily to her friends. Perhaps it was time to try something different.

What? Now? Get real! And as if she'd get the chance!

But for someone who had spent most of her life dreaming, and putting those dreams down on paper and canvas, there was no harm in looking, as she watched Kris mingle and charm. He wasn't predatory, and some of her single female friends were very pretty, nor was he condescending with the men. He was just a great guy…or he appeared to be. Perhaps he didn't have an agenda and she was just being neurotic, but appearances could be deceptive, Kimmie thought as she remembered Mike.

Around half an hour in, Kris was ready to leave. 'Do we have to go when you go?' Kimmie asked, concern building as she noticed how much her friends had relaxed since he'd arrived. They'd been distracted from her troubles by something new, and she was grateful for that because now they could really enjoy themselves without forcing the fun for her sake.

'Your friends don't have to go,' he said, 'but you do.'

'Me? I'm not going anywhere. I'm staying with my friends.'

'Then you can all leave,' Kris said flatly.

His tone was light and conversational, but the expression in his eyes said something different. 'Come on,' he prompted with a gesture.

Was she a puppy to be led away? She might be suffering the aftershock of betrayal, but she hadn't lost her mind completely.

'I'm not going anywhere,' she assured him, digging her feet into the sand.

Of all the reactions she might have expected, an easy smile was not on the list. 'Don't you want to come with me?'

A host of forbidden pleasures flew into her mind, but she had the sense to discard all of them. She'd thought Mike was safe, and look what had happened. Kris didn't even pretend to be the safe option, with that gladiator's body, tattoos and a single small gold hoop in his ear. He was danger personified.

Wasn't he exactly the type of distraction she needed right now? It seemed to work for her friends.

Because their emotions weren't battered and bruised, she reasoned. Standing close enough to Kris to imagine the heat of his sun-warmed body embracing her was warning enough. Warm, clean, spicy—strong white teeth, Hollywood pristine, with the fire of the devil in his eyes? That was everything she didn't need.

'I thought you might like to talk some more,' he said.

She ground her jaw. It wasn't like her to be indecisive, but it wasn't like her to take such an almighty risk, either.

'We'll just walk somewhere close by and talk,' he suggested.

Talking was safe, she persuaded herself as they set off down the beach.

Yes, but why would he take the trouble to do that? 'Where are we going?'

She turned to glance at her friends. They'd noticed her leaving the party, and they'd taken a pretty good look at Kris, who hadn't even tried to hide himself away, so she felt reasonably confident that she could handle this as they started to climb up the dune.

'Too fast for you?' he asked, stopping to wait for her to catch up. With his black stare fixed on her face and his firm mouth curving faintly, Kris was quite a sight, and surely he had to know the havoc he was creating in her fastidiously prepared wedding day body?

She was glad for the chance to catch her breath. Maybe talking to a stranger like Kris would sort things out in her head. There was so much emotion roiling around inside her it was like having a lava plug waiting to blow.

'Make like Scheherazade,' Kris suggested, curbing a smile. 'Keep me entertained and you'll buy more time on the beach for your friends.'

'As long as it's only talking,' she said warily.

'Obviously.'

'Okay then,' she agreed as they set off again.

'God, you're annoying,' she whispered under her breath as Kris's smile broke through his reserve. So why was she still here? Because there was annoying and then there was Kris, Kimmie concluded as he held out a hand to haul her up the last few yards of the sand dune.

Kimmie's resilience was something else. Stubborn to a fault, he'd never liked a pushover and she would push back. She was out of breath when they reached the top, so he waited before starting down the other side of the dune. Before they disappeared out of sight she shot one last look at her friends, as if to reassure herself they were still close by.

'Some people might expect a jilted bride to sit at home sobbing,' he observed, steadying her as she slithered down the slope.

'But I'm not at home,' she pointed out, 'and I've got guests to entertain.'

'You've succeeded, as far as I can tell, so stop beating yourself up.'

'Who says I'm doing that?'

'I believe I did.'

'So I can't hide anything from you?' she queried with a lift of her finely drawn brow.

'No,' he said flatly, 'so don't even try.'

He led the way to one of nature's indentations in the sand. 'This will do,' he said. 'Feel free to unburden yourself.'

'Just talking,' she said again with a warning look.

'There's nothing else on the table,' he assured her.

Who are you, just *Kimmie?* he wondered. *And where did you learn to stand up for yourself like this?* The unicorn inked on her shoulder backed up her story of being an artist, a creative, a dreamer, and not his type at all. He went for older, more experienced women who knew the score. They used him as he used them, for sex and pleasurable outings, no strings attached on either side.

'I am going to pull you up on something,' she said as they settled down in the dip of sand.

'Only one thing?' he murmured dryly, starting to get the hang of Kimmie's thinking.

'Yes. If you read the small print on the sign, it describes this area as a wildlife reserve accessible only by permission of the owner, so what are you doing here?'

'I have permission but, unfortunately, not on me at this moment.'

'As I can see,' she said, cheeks pinking up as she pointedly avoided looking at his almost naked body. 'It just doesn't seem fair that you can come here and we can't.'

'Change the subject,' he said.

'What do you mean?'

'I'm bored with that topic.'

'Oh, well, I'm very sorry about that—' She gasped as he caught hold of her. 'And what are you doing now?'

Staring into her eyes, he held her just far enough away for Kimmie to imagine he was going to kiss her. She was romantic enough to believe it and that could be useful if he decided to progress this. Thinking about his uncle's diktat that Kris should find a bride fast, it was hard not to laugh out loud. He couldn't imagine his uncle had someone like Kimmie in mind. Bright, independent and very much with a mind of her own, he doubted she'd see much merit in marrying him.

Marrying him?

What the hell was he thinking now? He didn't know her well enough. Yes, he could get to know her, and he had no doubt that would make his uncle happy. *Succession planning,* Theo Kaimos had said before Kris left Athens for Kaimos. *It's time you stopped tomcatting around and found yourself a decent woman.* Kris didn't want to disappoint the man who'd brought him up like a son, but he had pointed out that the type of woman his uncle had in mind didn't just drop out of the sky.

Maybe they washed up on a beach?

Dismissing that thought, he turned his attention back to Kimmie.

Kris hadn't kissed her, and now she felt such a fool because she'd been so sure he was going to. Worse, she'd been going to let him. Her emotions were all over the place. Was she destined to be a victim of circumstance forever, or would she grab hold of life again at some point and drive forward?

'Where are you going?' Kris asked as she stood up.

'Back to my friends.'

'But we haven't started talking yet.'

'Maybe I've changed my mind.'

'And maybe you shouldn't do that.'

He sprang up too, and his hands were gentle on her shoulders. Just for a moment she wanted to sink into that feeling. It felt so good to have someone strong who might actually listen to what she had to say, someone who might take hold of her if or when she was falling. But that was another fantasy, though this was what she'd been longing for all day, a quiet place and a chance to think things through. Getting away from people who knew her too well was actually a relief. However hard her friends tried to hide it, she knew they felt sorry for her and the last thing she needed was pity. What she needed was to work things out, get back on her feet, and get back out there fighting. Her plan to dance wildly and party like a demon until the sight of Mike and Janey going at it like rabbits had been ejected from her head was pathetic, and wouldn't have helped. It would just have made her feel worse.

And *this* wasn't a mistake? Kimmie thought as Kris's customary rock-hard expression softened a little in a way that suggested he might kiss her when he judged the moment right. Naturally her body thought this was a great idea, and only common sense was left behind.

'Are you okay?' he asked, seeing her frown.

There were so many answers to that question it was safer not to speak at all. When she stared into his eyes all her problems seemed to disappear. Kris was compelling in a way she'd never encountered before, which made it totally useless telling herself that, having spent all her adult life shying away from forming more intimate relationships, she was going to forget all her fears now.

'Are you frightened of sex? Is that why your fiancé was unfaithful to you?'

'Wow!' She drew her head back with surprise. 'You don't hold back, do you?'

Kris shrugged. 'It's a simple question.'

'And one you have no right to know the answer to.'

He conceded this with a dip of his head, but the steady beam of his eyes didn't let up.

'I think it's probably time I went back now,' she stated.

'If you want, or you can tell me more. It's entirely up to you. I'm in no hurry,' Kris assured her.

'What do you want to hear about?'

'You could start with your early childhood.'

'What are you? A shrink?'

'No, but I know which buttons to press. So tell me or don't. It's up to you. Shall we sit down again?' he suggested when she remained silently brooding.

'Can I trust you?' she said at last.

Kris shrugged. 'Time will tell. Meanwhile, what do you have to lose?'

'Not much,' she agreed with a humourless laugh.

'Then we'll begin.'

'I have a few questions for you first.'

'Shoot.' Leaning back on his elbows, he waited for her to begin.

'I just want to know—are you a local fisherman perhaps working as crew when fish are scarce?'

He burst out laughing.

'Are you or not?' she pressed.

Kris's eyes were still dancing with laughter. 'I'm your sultan and you're Scheherazade buying time for your friends, remember.'

'Like you said, I'm bored with that story.'

'Me too.' Resting back, he waited.

'I can't be long or my friends will send out a search party,' she warned.

'I doubt that somehow. They know where you are and who you're with.' Kimmie was changing her mind about telling him anything more, he guessed, and that was a shame. She had to want to tell him and if he didn't learn about her he couldn't pursue the admittedly wild idea that Kimmie might prove to be the answer to his uncle's request. 'Do you want to spoil their fun?'

'No,' she admitted. 'I don't.' She followed this by glancing in the direction of the music blowing on the wind in short, irregular bursts.

It must have occurred to Kimmie that she was with a man she hardly knew. It was his duty to re-assure her. *'Chapter One. Kimmie's Life Story...'* he murmured.

'Okay,' she murmured back.

'Talking things out is therapeutic,' he reassured.

It took a while for Kimmie to get into her stride, but eventually the fact that she was opening up to a relative stranger became less important than opening up. It was like lancing a wound. Once the pus came oozing out, it started to flow faster and faster, and with each new fact the telling became easier. And it wasn't all doom and gloom. She had lots of anecdotes about her childhood that made her laugh as she looked back.

He didn't laugh. He remained quite still, listening intently.

CHAPTER THREE

'So your first memory is...?'

'Staring at a brass poker while having my nappy changed,' she joked, 'but I'm not sure you want to hear that.'

He laughed. 'Moving on. Let's try for something else.'

'Okay, then... I'm in a dark room, crawling on the floor...'

'Crawling in your bedroom?' he prompted.

'No, I don't think so.' She screwed up her face as she thought back. 'It doesn't smell nice and there are empty bottles on the floor. It's sticky. I remember picking up a cigarette butt, though I didn't know what it was at the time. There was a lipstick stain on the end of it that made me think of my mother. I put it down again because it smelled nasty. And now I remember I was hungry... I wanted something to eat, and I'm cold—'

'Okay.' Shocked, he cut her off. 'Why don't we leave it there? I didn't mean you to relive a time when you were frightened and alone, and I apologise for pushing you. You must think me insensitive.'

'No, I think you're curious,' she said.

'This isn't a joke.'

She smiled ruefully. 'You're telling me. Or maybe I embellished the tale to keep your interest a little longer so the party could continue…?'

'I don't believe that for a minute,' he said, springing to his feet. 'Come on…let's go.'

'What have I done wrong?'

'Absolutely nothing,' he told Kimmie firmly. 'You've done nothing wrong.'

What about his uncle? What about his agreement to at least consider the suggestion that he, Kris, should get married and settle down?

He'd never found himself in a situation where scruples overruled his natural instinct to seduce, but by the time Kimmie had finished relating this first chapter of her life, where she'd clearly had a less than ideal childhood, he was committed to protecting her from further harm, and nothing else.

'So? How did I do?' she asked as she stood too. 'Are my stories good enough to keep your interest so we can let the party continue?'

'They're pretty good,' he said, feeling a pang of anger and pain on her behalf.

'Are you ready for the next instalment?'

'Honestly? Not right now.'

'I've bored you,' she said immediately.

'Far from it.' Having appeared so feisty when they'd first met, she now seemed vulnerable in the extreme. Cupping her face, he stared into her eyes. 'You're quite the survivor, Kimmie Lancaster.'

'And more than a match for you,' she assured him with gusto.

'Of that I've got no doubt,' he said as he released her and stood back.

He could buy anything on a whim, do anything at a moment's notice, but he couldn't match Kimmie. She was unique in a world of grasping insensitivity and he'd be a fool to let her go, but she was clearly a free spirit and he doubted anyone could tame her. That she'd been hurt so badly today had only added to her determination never to be tied down. There wasn't a chance she'd fall into his arms and marry him just because it suited his uncle. To produce the longed-for heir would be a lot harder than Uncle Theo imagined if Kris decided on Kimmie.

She'd killed any hope of seduction stone dead, which was good, Kimmie thought. Anything done in the heat of the moment while her emotions were all over the place could only be something to regret. Digging deep into her memory bank as, for some reason, she'd been tempted to do with a man she'd probably never see again, was as futile as dancing wildly on the beach.

When Kris pulled her into his arms, it was a total surprise. The kiss came when she least expected it, and was not what she expected from him at all. There was no pressure, no force, no sudden lunge; he just dipped his head and seduced her with his lips, his mouth lightly against hers. Drugging her with almost gentle kisses, her lips were tingling when he pulled away and she definitely wanted more. Her body urgently demanded more as Kris moved on to lace his fingers through her hair and lowered his head again, almost as though he'd heard her body's demands. The feeling was sensational, and allowed him to control the teasing kisses and deepen them at will. With each careful penetration her body ached, and he lengthened the kisses until the two of them were bound in a single unit of pleasure. This made her long for a far more intimate invasion, one that would make sensation consume her so she forgot everything else.

Pressing her body against his, she soon realised that Kris's mastery was everything she'd ever hoped for in a lover, and had given up any expectation of finding. Mike had always put himself first, and had been impatient with Kimmie's innate fear of intimacy. It was only extremely reluctantly that he'd agreed to Kimmie's request that they not sleep together until their wedding night. She should have known then that they were heading for disaster.

'You're shivering,' Kris noticed. 'Has something upset you? You can't expect me not to feel desire when I'm holding you so close. Are you having second thoughts?'

'None.' She was strong. She'd told Kris more about her early childhood than she'd ever told Mike. Even though she hardly knew him, Kris encouraged while Mike dictated—another piece of darkness that had crept up on her silently. Having braced herself for the wedding night, thinking if she could just jump that hurdle everything else would be all right, she knew now that Mike would never have been committed to their marriage. Naively, she'd thought he'd be a good partner, managing the business side of her work while Kimmie painted up a storm. Dreams were just that, she concluded. Childish fantasies. But this was different. Matching her strength against an equally firm-minded man was invigorating, not wearisome or depressing, and the one thing she badly needed to reinvigorate was her pep.

But that didn't mean losing her grip on reality. She knew nothing about Kris—where he called home, or if he had a family. He might have come from anywhere and could go back there just as fast.

'You're not married?' she asked suddenly.

'No, or even remotely entangled,' he reassured her.

To the deep regret of Uncle Theo, Kris mused silently, and he'd had no plans to change the status quo at the moment, though he did want Kimmie. Bringing her so close he could feel her heart racing against her chest, he sensed her hunger and also her fear. He was so much bigger than she was, though ironically they fit together perfectly. But his main concern was that she had never properly answered his question as to whether she was frightened of sex and, despite her passionate response to his kisses, he felt a hesitation deep inside her, which made him doubly determined not to overwhelm her.

Overwhelm Kimmie? With a lifetime of control

under siege, he was the one under pressure. He'd never experienced anything like it. The urge to claim her was eating him up inside. How could anything happen this fast? He didn't know her. She was a girl on a beach who had told him a few troubling stories. She could be lying about everything to win his sympathy in an attempt to trap him, and she wouldn't be the first.

'Kris?' she said, arranging the scarf she'd tied around her bikini so it covered her a little more. 'It's your turn to frown. I'm happy to go back.'

'No. There's no need to do that.'

She shrugged. 'The party will be winding down soon.'

Her voice was soft and musical. She was used to being hurt and that touched him. Turning her face to the sun, she closed her eyes as if to shut out the reality of a turbulent day. It was more than he could stand. He had to sample the smile on her kiss-bruised mouth. One kiss led to another until they were feasting on each other and he had to pull back.

'Ten minutes more,' she said, sinking back down on the sand.

As her kitten eyes flashed with something a world away from fear, he was gladly bewitched. This quirky, vulnerable woman was like no one he'd ever met. *She* was seducing *him*. Resting back on her elbows, she allowed her lush breasts to thrust forward so her nipples stood proudly erect. Her extraordinary purple-streaked hair brushed the sand and there was no mistaking the longing in her eyes. She was giving him a look as old as time. He didn't need prompting. His groin had tightened to the point of pain.

Stretching out his length beside her, he briefly considered the possibility of a set-up. It was an occupational hazard for rich and powerful men. Just because Kimmie was so different from the rest didn't automatically make her harmless, but his best guess was that she planned to use him to forget her ex-fiancé. What she clearly hadn't taken into account was how she'd feel about herself afterwards.

Decision made, he sprang to his feet. 'I'm taking you back.'

'Did I do something wrong?'

Surprise, hurt and bewilderment flashed behind her eyes in quick succession. It couldn't be helped. He wasn't a counsellor or Kimmie's keeper. Had she changed his thinking? Maybe. He'd never needed patience where seduction was concerned, but Kimmie was wounded and needed time to recover. They were both damaged by a past that had made him independent, always, and had made Kimmie a survivor too.

'You're taking me back to the party?' she asked uncertainly as he headed away from the beach.

'No. I'm taking you home.'

'To your home?'

'No, back to the guest house.'

This was a first for him. When he identified something he wanted he went straight for it, but Kimmie demanded a different approach. It was never easy to hold back and show the type of restraint she would require, but when had he ever embraced easy?

* * *

Now she felt worse than ever. Rejected twice in one day was too much for anyone. Labelling herself a naïve and pathetic failure, she scrambled to her feet. Overreaction? Probably, but her emotions were raw today. She shouldn't have gone so far, or told him so much. She shouldn't have kissed Kris because now she knew how that felt, and was equally certain that no other man could ever compare. If only she'd spared a moment to think how she'd feel afterwards, or that she was heaping humiliation upon humiliation on herself. Was she so unattractive? Had she bored him as she'd obviously bored Mike? Had telling Kris some of her life story, or at least a carefully edited version of it, been her worst mistake? Had kissing her been unpleasant for him, or had something else put him off? He'd seemed to enjoy the kisses, so perhaps it was a case of too much personal information. She'd found it dangerously easy to unburden all those memories to Kris. Would he yawn about it later? Would he laugh about it with his friends? She could only imagine Kris surging through life on a wave of approval, while she was still struggling to climb out of the mud.

That had to be it, Kimmie concluded as she checked her bottom was covered, and wished her bikini top was a little bit more concealing.

'We'll walk up the cliff,' Kris informed her, staring skywards to where the craggy rock face threw a shadow over the beach, 'and then I'll drive you back.'

'You've got a car up there?' She glanced at him with surprise.

'A house too.'

She went hot and then cold. It wasn't just her emotions that were in a mess. Her brain cells were crashing too. 'So this is your beach.'

Kris didn't answer. 'Should we make a start on the climb? Or I can take you back to your friends. Whichever you prefer.'

'You haven't answered my question.'

'No,' he said. 'I haven't. Nor have you answered mine.'

What the heck was happening? She needed time to think. Who was this man? Her suspicions were racing. Did she want to go back to her friends, or would she prefer to unscramble her thoughts in private? It had been good to escape their curiosity and pity, and not just because the distraction was Kris. The climb up the cliff would take all her energy, so there'd be no time for thinking or fretting, or wondering what Kris's motive was in being so considerate towards her.

'The walk will do you good,' he said as if confirming her thoughts.

'Like taking my medicine?' she suggested wryly as she glanced up the cliff.

'Like keeping you in that quiet place where you don't have to explain yourself to your friends,' Kris said with piercing intuition. 'And anyway,' he added in a lighter tone, 'I thought you liked adventure?'

'Why do you think that?'

'Gut instinct.'

'So you haven't had enough of me?'

He shrugged. 'I like a challenge.'

'So do I,' Kimmie admitted, 'but in this instance I'm going to tell my friends what I'm doing.'

'A wise precaution,' Kris agreed. 'We'll walk that way.'

Why not let this play out? She wasn't ready to let go of Kris yet. He was the best thing that had happened in a wretched day, and seemed in no hurry to get rid of her. She could go with him or not. Find out more about him, or spend the rest of her life wondering, *What if?*

'Before we set off there's that question you didn't answer,' she reminded him. 'You're not crew or a local fisherman, are you?' And when he chose to stare at her with a non-committal expression on his face, she stated with sudden certainty, 'You're the man who owns the island. You're Kristof Kaimos, CEO of Kaimos Shipping, said to be the richest man in the world. Unmarried, untouchable, and determined to remain unattached, according to the press, in spite of your uncle's best efforts to see you married off.'

'You seem to know a lot about me.'

Hot and cold had just become shards of ice and spears of fire piercing every inch of her. *Kris was Kristof Kaimos.* Incredible. Impossible. But very real.

'It's hard to avoid news of the super-rich,' she admitted with all the cool she could muster. 'Anyway, I feel quite safe now.'

'Meaning?' Kris probed, frowning.

'Meaning I can't imagine you would rope me in for the role of consort.'

He laughed out loud, a flash of strong white teeth against his burnished tan. 'You have such a romantic way of putting things,' he remarked. His stare burned into her as he looked down.

'I'm a bit worried that you haven't denied it,' she admitted, 'but I'm confident your selection of wife will come from a much more prestigious group of women than a jobbing artist could hope to join. As for being romantic? Believe me, I'd love to be romantic, but life made me wise up in a hurry.'

'We all make mistakes.'

'Even you, Kris Kaimos?' she challenged. 'Will you regret meeting me by tomorrow morning?'

'I can't possibly know until tomorrow comes.'

'You're good at evading questions, aren't you?'

'I'm a businessman.'

'I don't believe you've answered a single one of my questions,' Kimmie mused, 'but I suppose there is an upside to that. If your business fails, you could always consider becoming a politician.'

'My business won't fail.'

'No. I don't believe it will,' she agreed. 'With you at the helm, it wouldn't dare.'

Humour glinted briefly in Kris's eyes, but then he turned serious. 'Would you rather I made a pretence of feelings I don't have?'

'No, of course not. Most people would try to be

a little more diplomatic, but you won't even fudge the issue.'

'No, I won't,' he agreed.

Life had made them both cold fish, Kimmie concluded, and it was lonely in their ivory towers.

'Decision time,' he said. 'Stay with your friends, or come with me?'

'Friends first, then you,' she said.

'Okay. Let's do this.'

'Ready,' Kimmie confirmed.

CHAPTER FOUR

WITH HIS SUSPICIONS about Kimmie's motives temporarily laid to rest, attraction fired between them. She'd convinced him she had no idea who he was at first, and he needed no convincing that she was less than impressed by the trappings of wealth. This had been demonstrated by her casual dismissal of one of the finest superyachts in the world as a 'floating office block'. She amused him, aroused him and she interested him. He wanted to know more.

With no way to contact his people on board the *Spirit of Kaimos*, his security team was far more likely to send out a search party than Kimmie's friends, so he had to return to his house on the cliff to bring the team up to date. Then he'd drive Kimmie back to the guesthouse.

Waiting until she'd reassured her friends, he said goodbye to them, and he and Kimmie turned to head up the cliff.

'I want to paint you,' she said, surprising him, and not for the first time that day.

'Really?' he queried as they began the climb.

'Well, you know I'm an artist.'

'You did mention it.'

'The walk will give me chance to think about where I'd you'd like to sit. For preparatory sketches,' she explained.

'You decide that?'

'It doesn't have to be a battle of wills,' she joked. 'We can decide together.'

'How about here, staring out to sea?'

'Maybe…' She slanted him a smile.

'You've got my interest,' he prompted. She had a lot more than that. He'd never felt such a need to keep a woman close, so he could get to know her, really know her.

'And you've certainly got mine,' she said. 'You'll make a great subject.'

'With my manly physique and handsome face?'

'No,' she said, frowning, as she studied him closely. 'With those shadows you hide so well behind your eyes. Now, if I could capture them—'

'Come on,' he said brusquely, resenting her perceptive appraisal of him, 'or we won't make it to the top before sunset.'

Kris's expression had hardened. So it was all right for him to ask her questions. Interrogation of interesting prospects was his default setting, she guessed, but when it came to probing questions about his own life, he clammed up.

'Lead on,' she said lightly, 'and just this once I'll follow you.'

As Kris registered her comment with a grunt, she thought this was a crazy end to a crazy day, with no straightforward answers to the questions banging in her head. Why was he spending this time with her? Why would a man like Kristof Kaimos waste the best part of a day on a jilted bride?

Quite out of breath, she rested her hands on her knees as they reached the top of the cliff. When she finally straightened up, she exclaimed, 'Wow! What an amazing house.'

'You'd like to paint it?'

'Maybe,' she said again with a smile.

'I'm glad you approve.'

'I do approve. It's fabulous.'

'Thank you.'

They were outside some incredible gates, looking through. The property beyond was definitely exclusive.

'Does it make a difference now you know who I am?' he said as she stared like a child on a day out in London.

'Well, yes, of course it does,' Kimmie admitted.

Suspicion blazed in his eyes. 'Why?'

'It goes back to wanting to paint you,' she explained. 'You're not as straightforward as my other sitters.'

'And why is that?' Kris demanded, doubly suspicious.

'Because a painting of Kristof Kaimos would be worth a fortune on the open market, so that changes things quite a lot. A sketch of a local guy I met on a beach in Greece would be a lovely memento, and might feature in an exhibition one day, but even a preparatory sketch of the great Kristof Kaimos would be worth a lot of money. I can't just go ahead and do one, then show it and sell it, because that would be taking advantage of you.'

'You'd care that much?'

'Don't you think I have any scruples?'

Unconcerned that she was affronted by his comment, Kris shrugged. 'What if I gave you permission?'

'Would you do that?'

She couldn't believe it. A world of possibilities flashed through her head. It would be dishonest not to admit that a commission from Kristof Kaimos would be an enormous boost for her career.

'Earlier you said you had a project to get off the ground,' he said as he used fingerprint recognition to open the gate. 'Would this help you to do that?'

'Of course it would,' Kimmie admitted. Hope and excitement soared as she explained, 'It's been a dream of mine for years, to set up a scholarship to help young artists get a start—maybe go to college or take extra lessons, so they get the chance to show the world their artwork. If you do allow me to paint you, the proceeds of that sale would really get things moving.' She paused and frowned.

'What's wrong now?' he pressed.

She shook her head. 'I'd still feel as if I was exploiting you.'

'Not if I agree to be exploited,' he said as the pedestrian gate swung open to admit them. 'Which I do,' he confirmed to her amazement, adding, 'I might even buy the painting for my uncle. He'd love that.'

'Your uncle?' Kimmie's mind raced to plug the gaps in her scant knowledge of Kristof Kaimos. 'The uncle that wants you to get married?'

'That's just gossip,' he scoffed. 'After you,' he said, inviting her into the grounds.

'I didn't mean to offend you.'

'You didn't. It's just that I have one uncle, and he's very special. I consider him to be my father. He brought me up. You could say he saved me.'

So that was where the shadows came from. She didn't prompt. She didn't dare. She didn't want a return to the rigidly aloof Kris, who shut her out so effectively.

They had started to walk up a beautifully groomed path between formal gardens, lovingly tended and vibrant with banks of colourful flowers. It was the perfect setting for relaxation and easy conversation, but Kimmie had a feeling that Kris felt he'd said too much, and the rest of the walk would be conducted in silence if she didn't say something.

'What happened to your parents?' she asked. There was no point dressing it up. There was a trauma to be uncovered and understood, if she had a hope of putting any depth into a painting of the man.

Was painting Kris the only reason she wanted to know more about him?

'If you don't want to tell me—'

'No, I do,' he said a little curtly, perhaps in the

hope of shutting her up. 'My parents loved partying, and one day they partied so hard they forgot they had a child. My uncle rescued me from the streets of Athens, where I was found wandering. There's only me and Theo left now.'

There wasn't much she could say to that. It was so much worse than she'd imagined. No wonder Kris withdrew behind his barricades. He must have been doing that since he was a child. She hadn't anticipated uncovering such a wretched similarity between them. The few newspaper reports she could recall had mentioned Kristof Kaimos's unparalleled drive and his almost fiendish dedication to his business. Now she knew why he felt so strongly about showing his gratitude to an uncle who meant so much to him. Kris would probably spend the rest of his life doing so. She could really empathise because, like Kris, since childhood Kimmie had determined she would never be a victim again.

It wasn't really possible to uncover all the onion layers of a person on first meeting them, she reflected as they approached the entrance to Kris's house. There was just chemistry, or animal instinct, that drew one person to another, but maybe there was such a thing as fate, and maybe fate had a reason for throwing them together, although—and she had no illusion about the likelihood of Kris even considering this—she had no intention of becoming his convenient bride, any more than Kris would leap across the gulf dividing them to get down on one knee.

And weren't these crazy thoughts on the day she'd

been jilted at the altar? Time to get real, Kimmie concluded, as Kris strode past the house, quickening his step so she had to almost run to keep up with him. Perhaps he couldn't wait to get rid of her now. He obviously regretted sharing as much as he had. He would think it a sign of weakness to show off his scars. Just as Kimmie felt hers had never really healed, Kris didn't like to admit to the same.

'I love your house,' she said, hoping to ease the tension that had grown between them. She wasn't completely naïve, and had expected a billionaire's roost to be off-the-scale fabulous, but this was something else. The sheer size and splendour of the building, enhanced by various add-ons like a line of tennis courts and a swish pavilion. There was the competition-sized pool and, of course, the indispensable helipad. All of it made the gulf between them even more unbridgeable. Painter and subject didn't require parity between them, she reminded herself; all that was required was a steady hand and, in the case of painting Kristof Kaimos, an even steadier nerve.

'Painting your estate could be my life's work,' she said carelessly as thoughts of holding a paintbrush in her hand again took hold.

'It's always lovely here at sunset,' Kris observed with what was almost a dismissive gesture as he strode on.

He was missing so much, Kimmie thought, longing to make Kris linger so he could see things as she did with her artist's eyes. Everything was subtly lit so the gardens glowed lush green, while glittering water features competed with ancient statuary. Beyond these, seemingly endless miles of ocean stretched to unseen horizons. What a place to make the imagination fly. It was glorious.

She turned to look at Kris, who'd stopped walking to wait for her, and wondered what she was doing here with this man. A more relevant question might be—what was Kris doing here with her? What did he want with her? If he wanted the obvious he could have made his move on the beach, but he'd behaved like a gentleman. Because he knew her emotions were churning, she reasoned, and Kris was too big a man to take advantage of a woman in distress.

'What?' he prompted, seeing she was distracted.

'Oh, a helipad,' she said as if she'd never seen such a thing before. Let him think her naïve and unworldly. Better that than he read some of her thoughts.

'And over there,' he said with humour in his voice, pointing, 'is a runway for my private jet.'

'Only one?' she queried, tongue in cheek.

Kris's lips twitched and he almost smiled, but she had to be careful. She liked him a lot. Too much, maybe, and that was dangerous for her bruised and battered heart.

'Do you play?' he asked as they passed the tennis courts.

'I like to lob a few balls back into court,' she admitted dryly, but when he smiled she told the truth. 'My hand–eye coordination is lousy.'

'I'm surprised,' he said. 'You being an artist…'

'I don't like running.'

'Away from anything,' he guessed. 'How about swimming? That would cool you down.'

If only it was that easy. Her temperature rose just looking at Kris.

'You could stay over,' he offered. 'Guest accommodation,' he said before her heart could start pounding with alarm.

'That's a kind offer, but no, thank you. I'd better get back.'

'Yes,' he agreed, 'you'd better.'

She couldn't read anything into the tone of his voice and, even if she had, she would probably be guilty of overreacting. Her emotional foundations were still rocking, and her decision-making processes were shot to hell. But why ask her to stay over? Was Kris just curious about her, as she was about him, or did he want to take a closer look at her like a scientist with an interesting project in mind? With his uncle's interesting project in mind, she amended. Or was that reading too much into this?

'It must take an army of staff to run a place like this,' she commented, in an attempt to distract them both as they headed around the back of the house. 'You must be heavily outnumbered.'

He stopped dead and turned to stare at her. 'You have an interesting take on almost everything, Ms Lancaster.'

Kimmie shrugged. 'From my perspective it's an

obvious comment. I have one room with a bath-room attached…and no staff,' she added, pulling a comic face.

Kris almost smiled again. 'Do you envy me?'

'Envy you?' Kimmie exclaimed. 'Certainly not. I feel sorry for you, actually. I don't know how anyone who could make a house this size a home.'

'A home?' Kris queried, frowning.

'Yeah, you know, one of those things people live in and love, and make cosy and comfortable.' Didn't everyone need somewhere like that to hunker down in when they were off-duty? Kimmie's tiny home fitted the bill. It might not be grand like this, and it might only be rented rather than owned by her, but it was somewhere to snuggle up in and feel safe. 'Don't you ever get lonely here?'

'Lonely? Why would I be lonely?' Kris queried with surprise.

'I imagine that army of staff has better things to do than mix with you in their downtime, and contact with people is important…isn't it? It is to me. I work on my own, so I love to meet people.'

'I have all the contact I need with humanity in my working life,' Kris assured her coolly. He sounded slightly irritated and she guessed no one had ever questioned whether the material things his success had supplied him with had also brought him the one thing that really mattered, which was contentment.

'Why would I need a *cosy* home, as you put it?'

he queried. 'If I want something smaller I'll stay in a hotel.'

He just didn't get it. With property across the world, how could he? What she meant was—where was his anchor? Where was the place Kris called home? This vast residence was more like a luxury resort than a permanent roost.

'What happens when you get married?' she asked, and immediately regretted the question. But she pressed on. 'How on earth will you make this place inviting for a wife?'

Kris's chin jerked up as if she'd said something outlandish. Well, she had. She'd mentioned the *M* word, and shouldn't she, of all people, steer clear of that?

'That will be my wife's job, surely?' he said coolly.

'No equality here, then?'

Kris was not in the mood for any more teasing, and she had just ruined the evening with her big mouth. 'I just thought you might take an interest...'

'I do take an interest,' Kris assured her. 'I have an army of designers working on the house. Perhaps you'd like to see the artist's studio?'

Touché. 'The what?'

'The artist's studio,' he repeated.

She had to remind herself that a house this size could have pretty much anything: concert hall, artist's studio, theatre in the garden, football pitch, concert arena, and she had to stop jumping to conclusions and give Kris a break.

'Almost as if it were meant to be,' Kris added,

paying her back, she was sure, as he slid her a hot sideways look. 'My house isn't so vast and boring now, is it?'

'I'm impressed,' she admitted.

'In fact, this house used to belong to a very successful artist,' he explained.

Kimmie gasped at the name.

'There's quite a community of artists on Kaimos,' Kris revealed. 'Something to do with the light, I'm told.'

The more she learned about Kristof Kaimos, the more she wanted to know about him—about the real man, not the man the press reported on; he as a hollow shell, a billionaire like so many others, while Kris was unique and so, *so* intriguing. Filling her mind with images was all part of the artist's job. If she could learn what lay beneath the carapace of Kristof Kaimos, wildly successful billionaire, she could add texture to the strong lines of his face and flesh to his character. Understanding how he lived and why he lived a certain way was all part of that.

As they approached the line of garages housing countless high-value vehicles, she noticed for the first time that the sun was fading and had turned the stonework a pleasing shade of dusky chalk pink.

'Have I been out that long?' she exclaimed on an incredulous sigh. Suddenly she felt bone-weary. It had been the longest and most turbulent of days.

'Time for bed,' Kris prescribed as she smothered a yawn.

'Yes,' she could only agree. 'But I'd love to see

the artist's studio one day…if it's not too much trouble for you?'

'No trouble at all,' he insisted. 'I can always get someone to show you around.'

Oh.

But now she didn't want to go back to the guest house. The thought of being alone in that room when she should have been sharing a room with her husband tonight was confusing and worrying, even though Mike and Janey had swiftly packed up and left. She didn't want to be with Mike, but she didn't want to be alone either. After a horrible start to the day, she'd enjoyed being with Kris. She'd enjoyed the banter between them, and being able to forget. And she'd enjoyed his kisses…especially his kisses. Would he kiss her goodnight…on the cheek, on the lips? She didn't know what she wanted. Well, actually, that wasn't true. She did. The urge to paint complex, interesting, challenging Kris had never been greater.

She could sketch from memory, Kimmie reassured herself as Kris walked up to his sleek black SUV and opened the passenger door. And she'd choose a background to suit. It was time for both of them to return to their ivory towers: Kris here in his fabulous beach house, and Kimmie in the artist's cave, painting.

Didn't she want to see Kris again? Of course she did. Then she might have to make the first move. And what would he say to that? she wondered as he started the engine and released the brake. It was impossible to read his expression. As far as Kimmie was concerned, if she pushed her dreams to their ultimate conclusion it would mean this wasn't over yet and had only just begun.

CHAPTER FIVE

BACK AT THE GUEST HOUSE, to her absolute amazement, Kimmie slept like a baby that night. She thought it incredible after the events of the previous day. Waking slowly, she turned over to stare at the ceiling, where various scenes played out. Some were good, some were bad and some were truly spectacular. Had Kristof Kaimos really kissed her? She touched her lips and traced the tender skin where his stubble had abraded her. Kristof Kaimos had definitely kissed her. She had been thoroughly kissed. Astonishing, after the way yesterday had started.

She hadn't been able to judge his mood when he drove her home last night, other than to say he was the perfect gentleman. And of course some wicked, carnal imp inside her had taken the opportunity to make her long for Kris to introduce her to those pleasures she'd only dreamed about. That he'd do so with consummate skill wasn't in doubt, and made her longing for him all the keener. Fears she'd had in the past were redundant where Kris was concerned. If he made love as he kissed, that was to say sensitively, tenderly and passionately, it wouldn't be terrifying; it would be amazing. And for someone whose only knowledge of sex was hearing her mother scream when her father forced himself on her, Kimmie didn't have any reassuring memories to cling to, and only Kris's kisses to suggest that a mutual desire could and should be different.

This was something she should have thought more about when she'd accepted Mike's proposal but, buoyed up on a wave of euphoria at the success of her exhibition, she hadn't thought it through. Later, when Mike's impatience at her being frigid, as he'd flung at her and he'd handled her rather clumsily, hurting her, she'd had to pull away and tell him that the reason she was holding back from sleeping with him was because she was saving herself for the all-important wedding night, when the truth was she was just plain scared to have sex with him.

Thank goodness Kris respected women or she'd be lying here with more than her heart bruised. Snuggling down to enjoy the other good things about the night, she relived his kisses again. She'd never be able to kiss another man without comparing him to Kris. Then she thought about him steering the SUV around the narrow, winding lanes of Kaimos. She'd had no idea hands and arms could be so sexy…and she couldn't wait to paint them, of course, and from memory if she had to. She wouldn't forget a single detail of a man who had entered her life so unexpectedly on what had been the worst day possible. But then, when they'd got back to the guest house, he had said nothing as he sprang down from the SUV and came around to open her door.

One perfunctory kiss on the cheek was all she'd got and then he was gone, roaring off into the distance without so much as a backward glance.

Time to get real, Kimmie thought as she slipped out of bed. Half a fun day after a morning of catastrophe did not a romance make. No doubt she'd entertained Kristof Kaimos for a while, but she was sure there wouldn't be a second meeting.

But she'd been too tired to close the shutters last night, so it wasn't all bad because now she felt uplifted just staring out. What an amazing view! And his mega-yacht was still out there. For some reason, that reassured her, though Kris could be anywhere. He might even have gone back to Athens by now, or left for what she was sure would be one of his many residences or offices around the world. Did that mean he wouldn't keep his promise to show her the artist's studio? He'd actually said he'd get someone to show her around, and that wasn't the same thing at all.

Having taken a shower in the tiny bathroom attached to her room, Kimmie switched off the water, grabbed a towel, swaddled her body and tried not to think about Kris.

Well, that went well, Kimmie concluded as she padded back to the window to stare at his yacht. Her nipples were standing to attention just thinking about him. They were far more optimistic than she was. She stared down the road but there was no sign of Kris. And it was far safer for her heart if he didn't come back. She wasn't ready for any more excitement.

Oh, yes, she was. Life would be dull without it. Kris had taken the discarded, muddled daub of yesterday and given it form and purpose. She definitely wasn't ready to let go of that yet.

Turning away from the window, she rubbed her hair dry with a towel and thought about Kris. Strike that. She was thinking about her next composition, which would obviously feature Kristof Kaimos. She would start work on it as soon as she returned to London. She couldn't waste time on regret. Whatever life threw at her, she had always fought back. This wedding farce and then the meeting with Kris were just bigger hurdles than usual. The sooner she returned to work, the faster she could set up that scholarship fund.

Kris could be a sponsor. Why not?

She wouldn't dream of asking him, that was why not. It was just one more way of taking advantage of him because of his money.

Not if she wrote to him, together with a dozen or so more likely donors. And, in the unlikely event that she saw him again, she could ask him?

Hmm. Maybe. Maybe not.

'You look a lot better this morning,' Kyria Demetriou exclaimed with pleasure, advancing to give Kimmie a hug when she entered the dining room. 'Your face is glowing.'

'Is it?' Kimmie touched her cheek then blushed, wondering if Kris's stubble might have caused any redness. 'We all want to thank you for the delicious food. We had a wonderful picnic.' Of which she hadn't eaten a crumb, being otherwise occupied, Kimmie remembered, blushing furiously again. 'None of it was wasted. My friends enjoyed every crumb.'

Kyria Demetriou gave her an amused look, as if she knew more than she was saying. 'Now you're feeling better, I want you to know there's a fiesta tonight in the village. It's a traditional night, with folk music, local food and dancing, and I feel sure you'll enjoy it.'

'I know I will,' Kimmie enthused.

'We will all go,' Kyria Demetriou informed her. 'Everyone on the island will be there.'

Including Kris? Kimmie's heart pounded.

'You should take your sketch pad,' Kyria Demetriou encouraged, distracting her momentarily.

'That's a good idea.' Kimmie would be leaving the island soon, and tonight's celebration was the best chance she was going to get to record every impression she could. Hopefully there'd be enough to fuel a new exhibition.

The day passed slowly and, as expected, there was no sign of Kris. Kimmie's friends tried their best to distract her, and she played along. It was time to move past everything that had happened in Kaimos, and finally accept that Kristof Kaimos had better things to do than waste his time on a jilted bride and a simple village party. There was no chance he would surprise her there tonight, she managed to convince herself.

* * *

Kris spent the day mulling over the events of the previous day. It had been an incredible encounter with Kimmie, but a chance meeting following hot on the heels of an unreasonable request from the uncle to whom he owed everything was not a guarantee of anything. If anyone had suggested Kimmie as a suitable wife before he'd met her, he would have shot them down in flames. He didn't know her. She didn't know him. He'd seen her at the worst time possible.

And yet she had cast a very unique spell on him.

Why? She was strong, but also emotionally vulnerable. Right now she didn't know what she wanted. Yet, for all these reasons to step back and let her go, something nagged at him that said he shouldn't.

He spoke to his uncle later that day and admitted that he'd met *a prospect*, as his uncle hopefully referred to Kris's non-existent list of potential brides. 'Seriously, don't get your hopes up,' Kris had warned, but Uncle Theo wasn't listening.

'You should have sealed the deal by now,' his uncle insisted. 'It's not like you to hang around.'

'I only met her yesterday,' Kris was forced to patiently point out.

'And?' his uncle demanded.

'And she's bruised,' he said simply.

There was silence between Athens and Kaimos for quite a while after that, and then his uncle murmured, 'Dangerous.' He went on to spoil this brief show of empathy by saying, 'Sympathy can cloud a person's judgement. It's not like you to be so subjective, Kristof. Why are you suddenly allowing feelings to get in the way? I've never known you like this before.'

'Well, don't take it for a good sign,' Kris advised.

'You'll have to change tactics,' his uncle instructed. 'Do whatever it takes. I need to know you have an heir, Kristof. Woo her with sweet words and expensive gifts. That should do it,' his uncle finished with a triumphant flourish.

Kris was forced to curb a smile at this point. 'You haven't met Kimmie. She isn't impressed by wealth.'

'She's a saint?' his uncle demanded in a sceptical voice.

'She knows who I am, and it doesn't seem to make a difference,' Kris explained as Kimmie's combative gaze swam into his mind.

'That's only what she's showing you on the outside,' his uncle assured him. 'Who knows what she's really thinking?'

'Is that how you felt about my aunt when you two first met?'

The silence was deafening, and Kris knew he'd overstepped the mark. His uncle had been passionately in love with his wife, Kris's aunt, for more than forty years, but sometimes Uncle Theo needed reminding that other people had feelings too.

Even Kris?

Sitting here in his study at the beach house, he remembered shifting uncomfortably at that point, and longing to put down the phone. The last thing he had intended was to upset the man to whom he owed so much. After the call, it occurred to him he could have it all. Practical arrangements would have to come first, but as neither he nor Kimmie was exactly familiar with the trope of love, he couldn't see a problem.

Except for the fact that she was a true romantic?

No, no, no—she was an intelligent woman. It would not be a case of lavishing gifts on Kimmie, but employing calm reason and winning her trust. Others might see the gifts he bought them as fair exchange for their time, but Kimmie was not only likely to return any gifts he gave her, but would expect more from him emotionally than he was willing or able to give…

He had almost talked himself out of pursuing another encounter with Kimmie when her beautiful face flashed into his mind. Quirky, unpredictable, passionate Kimmie, bruised and damaged by life, but she always bounced back. What a woman. What a match for him. Feisty and independent, and so scorching hot he had to have her. Kimmie was everything he'd ever wanted and more.

At what cost?

Previous partners couldn't do enough for him in the bedroom, which was all that was required of them, but when it came to finding a wife…someone to spend time with, talk to and get to know, to care deeply about, a woman with whom he could build a family…

Forget it! He didn't have his uncle's talent where that was concerned.

* * *

A wonderfully sunny afternoon faded into a spectac-ular sunset as Kimmie and her friends left for their various rooms at the guest house to get ready for the fiesta in the village. The blood-red sky threw Kris's ship, the *Spirit of Kaimos*, into sharp relief, taunt-ing her as Kimmie stared out of her bedroom win-dow. There'd been no sign of him and, far from that being a relief, she felt as if a dead weight had lodged in the pit of her stomach. She looked forward to the celebration and hoped it would be a distraction. If nothing else, it would be a great send-off for the wed-ding guests, and her friends deserved nothing less.

Finding something suitable to wear wasn't so hard as her simple wedding trousseau, bought on the high street, remained untouched. She settled on a white cotton summer dress, which she teamed with flat sandals, before brushing her hair until it sprang around her shoulders like an angry purple storm cloud. She *was* angry. Mike had let everyone down, and hadn't even had the decency to show his face to apologise, or to make any sort of explanation to their friends.

Put him behind you! You don't have to think about Mike again.

Correct. Thus armed, she left her room and jogged downstairs to join the others. Kyria Demetriou's gen-erosity in wanting to introduce them around in the village was a great opportunity, and Kimmie made sure to take her sketch pad. Confident she'd find endless inspiration for her paintings, she'd work on pre-paratory sketches until she ran out of lead.

And Kris?

Forget about him too!

Could she? What if she saw him in the village with someone else? Someone sophisticated and beautiful—the type of companion she imagined he should have.

Suck it up.

Determined to put on a buoyant and optimistic front, she reached the foot of the stairs and stopped dead. There was no mistaking that voice. *Kris was here.* Her heart was beating so fast by the time she reached the door of the communal sitting room, she could hardly breathe.

But she could breathe, and she would…steadily, Kimmie told herself firmly as she walked into the room. She could handle this and any situation.

Could she, indeed?

Had she really thought she was ready to see Kris again? Why was she standing rooted to the spot, staring at him as if he was the only person in the room? Because there was no preparation possible for the sight of Kristof Kaimos contained in a very small room when he took up every inch of space with his personality alone. It didn't help that her friends were staring fixedly at Kimmie, waiting to see her reaction.

Move! And be quick about it. Say something!

'How nice to see you again,' she said politely, walking forward with her hand outstretched like a character out of *My Fair Lady*.

Nice? Kris was standing with his jeans-clad hips propped against the wall. *Nice?* He looked even more like that Titan from myth and legend tonight. He was so hot she needed a bucket of iced water to tip over herself. The worst of it was that a nervous smile seemed to have fixed itself to her trembling mouth.

He had no mercy. Straightening up, he towered over her and, right on cue, her body responded.

Yes, please, and as soon as you like, flashed through her mind. Forget her fear of sex. She couldn't fight the primal imperative of facing this big, potent male. And she didn't want to.

Because she was still suffering from the rebound response, Kimmie's killjoy inner caution warned.

And it got worse. When Kris's big fist closed around her hand, all she could think about was him touching her, kissing her, and progressing those kisses until...

'Good to see you again,' he murmured, sounding faintly amused, as if he could read every damning word in her mind.

Dressed casually in snug-fitting jeans that revealed far too much of what she remembered of his incredible body, he took her breath away. Far from being cool and collected as she had determined to be if he attended the fiesta tonight, she was staring back at him like some ingénue idiot. There was no getting around the fact that she wanted Kris to be the one to remove her fear of physical intimacy for good. She couldn't imagine trusting anyone else. How crazy was that when she didn't even know him?

'Are you ready to leave?' he prompted, his mouth tugging up in a sexy half-smile.

Right now, she wasn't sure what she was ready for, only that she wanted to be with Kris. Determined not to be thrown by his darkly amused manner, she turned to speak to Kyria Demetriou. 'I'm really looking forward to our night out. Thank you so much for arranging this.'

'Kristof did most of the arranging,' Kyria Demetriou revealed to Kimmie's surprise, and now their elderly host was beaming at Kris like a proud mother.

Kris's intent eyes caught hold of Kimmie's stare and held it firmly in his. She could only hope her eyes were as eloquent as his when it came to her earnest desire to smack him. She might want him, but not on any and all terms. She knew he was playing her like a big cat with a mouse, and now the entire room was holding its breath and it took Kyria Demetriou to break the tension. 'We'd better go now,' she said matter-of-factly, 'or all the best tables will be taken.'

Kimmie speared a look at Kris. Couldn't the local billionaire do anything about that? Surely Kristof Kaimos received special treatment on the island he owned.

The lift of one sweeping ebony brow and a lazy, mock scolding look informed her in no uncertain terms that Kris expected to be treated like any other man on the island, no better, no worse. Brownie points duly awarded, she consented to return his smile, with the predictable result that he held her gaze for far too long and her heart raced off the scale.

'We'll stop by the fiesta,' he announced to the room at large, with a brief glance at Kimmie. 'Then Kimmie and I will go on to my house, where I promised to show her the artist's studio.'

'Will we?' Kimmie challenged.

Everyone fell silent until one of her friends piped up, 'Is that the same as showing her your etchings?'

Kris took this surprisingly well. 'Who knows?' he said enigmatically.

CHAPTER SIX

IT WAS ONLY thanks to Kyria Demetriou, once again stepping between Kris and Kimmie, that their latest stand-off was finally broken. It was like something out of a comic black-and-white movie. One moment everyone in the room was motionless, staring avidly at Kimmie and Kris, and the next they were stampeding for the door.

'Allow me,' Kris insisted, assuming sentry duty. 'I hope you will allow me to escort you to the village, Kyria Demetriou?'

'I'd be delighted,' Kimmie's elderly host replied with the warmest of smiles.

Kimmie didn't miss Kris's raised brow as she trooped past him with her friends, or the curve of his lips when he noticed her fixed facial expression. *Game on,* she thought, swivelling around to flash him one last challenging glance.

Game on? Seriously? So soon after you were jilted, almost at the altar? Are you suddenly a seasoned campaigner? Admit it, Kimmie, you don't know anything about the game of love.

This wasn't a game; it was survival, Kimmie argued with her inner critic. What was she supposed to do? Give up? Retire from life? Let Mike win?

Kimmie's friends swallowed her up in their group as they set out on foot for the short walk to the town square and, as they clustered around her like a guard of honour, she could feel their support and love, and their curiosity too at the surprising chemistry that had obviously flared between Kimmie and a man who was literally a legend in his own lifetime. She had to be the only one amongst them who didn't expect anything to come of their surprise encounter.

There was no need to worry about bagging a good table. One of the best at the front of the restaurant had been reserved for them. The manager rushed to greet their group and make them all feel welcome, though Kimmie noticed that he offered an especially warm greeting to Kris.

'These are yours, I believe,' Kyria Demetriou told Kimmie as she put a sketch pad and pencils into her hand. 'I think you were so shocked back at the guest-house when you saw Kristof that you left them behind, but I know you'll need them tonight because here is where life and art will be combined.'

What did that mean? Kimmie wondered as she stared at the familiar tools in her hand.

'Sketch everything you see,' Kyria Demetriou advised, 'and then you will have that exhibition I know you long for. Life goes on,' she whispered.

There was a special type of kindness and understanding in Kyria Demetriou's eyes that told Kimmie she would never look back on her time in Kaimos with bitterness, and would only ever remember the island and its people in the warmest and most optimistic terms. It was a feeling she hoped to convey in her next exhibition.

'Don't allow anyone to hold back your dreams,' Kyria Demetriou went on as they prepared to take their seats at the table. 'Everything you want to take with you from Kaimos can be yours, because you can sketch it, record it and hold it tightly in your heart.'

'I will,' Kimmie promised as her elderly friend left her side to take her place at the head of the table. It was wonderful to have friends, and this was an amazing opportunity, Kimmie thought as she gazed around. The square was so vibrant with life and music, and with colour, light, good food and camaraderie, and everyone was so upbeat and friendly. If only she could capture the mood... She started sketching and was soon completely lost in her interpretation of the scene.

'Hard at work already?'

She didn't need to look up to know Kris was standing behind her when she could feel him in every fibre of her being.

'Hi...' She kept her head bent low over her work in case her feelings for him started flashing in her eyes like big neon signs.

'You're good…very good,' he murmured as he moved and came to sit across from her at the table.

She laughed, and finally lifted her head. 'You can't see my sketches properly upside down.' Predictably, her heart began to thunder a tattoo the moment she stared into his eyes.

'I've been standing behind you for the past ten minutes, so I've got a pretty good idea what they look like the right way up,' he argued with that faint sexy smile that made her inexperienced body melt. 'You must have completed half a dozen line drawings in that time, but you were so absorbed in your work you didn't notice me. Should I be offended?' Kris asked.

'I'm not ignoring you,' she said, staring into eyes that were glinting with amusement. 'I'm sure I'll find a small space somewhere in the sketch pad to record a quick line drawing of you, but you'll have to wait your turn,' she teased. 'This is such a wonderful scene. I don't want to miss anything.'

'What makes you think I can wait?'

His mouth had tugged up at one corner in a way she found irresistible. She would definitely have to remember that look when she sketched him.

The square was a distraction with its blaze of fairy lights and the brightly dressed crowd, but Kris in profile as he turned to speak to a friend was quick to capture her attention. But how to translate that incredible bone structure, and those amazingly expressive eyes and mouth, on paper with just a few sparse lines? As a warm-up she sketched a proud mother pushing a pram with another little girl clutching her hand.

'Okay?'

She refocused on Kris as he asked the question. He sounded concerned, and only then did she realise that her face had set in a wistful mask. True, she couldn't remember anyone wanting to hold her hand when she was a little girl, but she couldn't let those feelings show. What was the point when she couldn't change the past? And when the future was hers to grasp.

'I just need to record this so I don't forget,' she said.

Leaning over the table to take a look, he said, 'I can almost imagine what that woman's thinking.'

'Go on,' Kimmie prompted. She was intrigued to find that Kris didn't just see a snapshot but looked beyond the image, as she did, and she was keen to hear what he had to say, to see if they thought the same.

'She wishes she could stay out late with her husband to have a romantic evening,' he began, which was enough in itself to send shivers spinning down Kimmie's spine as their thoughts were so similar. 'But she also wants her children to have a good time and that's why she's frowning, because she can't work out how to combine the two.'

'That's exactly what I thought when I started sketching her,' Kimmie admitted.

'And you convey those thoughts extremely well,' Kris confirmed with a long look into her eyes.

'Thank you.' She wanted to say more, but her

entire body had heated up under Kris's penetrating stare and a reckless word might betray her longing for him. *Sometimes, saying thank you is enough*, she remembered wryly.

'And that man over there,' Kris said, pointing across the square. 'He's in a desperate hurry to sell his sticky cakes, so he can ditch the stall and have some fun.'

'You're right,' she said, smiling. 'You read people too.'

'I have to in my line of work.'

Another steady look made her wonder what Kris was thinking. Was she an open book to him? There was no relief from his scrutiny. They were only inches apart. The noise of people enjoying themselves simply faded away, until there was nothing but the two of them staring deep into each other's eyes.

'And where do I stand in your analysis of potential subjects for my sketch book?'

'You're at a crossroads,' Kris observed thoughtfully. When she didn't answer this, he pressed, 'Well? How did I do?'

'I'm not sure I understand what you mean,' she lied.

'I think you do,' Kris argued. 'I can read you, and you're standing at those crossroads right now, with life pulling you in different directions.

'You should stick to shipping,' she scoffed. 'Unless you want a crystal ball for Christmas.'

Kris was about to answer when someone attracted his attention and he turned away. Kimmie felt as if a weight had been lifted from her shoulders. She didn't want to be under the microscope. She wasn't ready for that. At the same time, while Kris was distracted she missed him. She missed his brooding interest. There was no hope for her, Kimmie concluded as the food arrived, and now no chance for anyone to speak as everyone helped to pass the food around.

Eating presented her with more problems. Eating was sexy. And Kris was a big man, so their knees brushed beneath the table. The table was rammed. They were bound to touch, Kimmie told herself firmly.

'Forgive me,' Kris said eventually, when the last person waiting to speak to him had finally retreated to their table to eat.

'For what?'

'For ignoring you. I've been away quite some time, so there's a lot of catching up to do.'

'No problem. I didn't realise how hungry I was, so if you ignored me, I didn't notice.'

'You noticed,' he assured her in a way that made her body yearn for more than sweet honey cakes.

With a shrug, she wiped her hands and picked up her sketchbook. The chemistry between her and Kris was extraordinary and compelling. And it would continue to do its dangerous work with or without her cooperation, she accepted, pencil poised.

'You've stopped sketching,' Kris remarked.

'Excuse me while I study my subject.'

Who was she trying to kid? She didn't need to

study Kris when every detail of his face—and at least 90 per cent of his body—was firmly etched on her mind.

'What do you see when you look at me? Apart from the shadows behind my eyes, I mean,' he added with a slight quirk at one corner of his firm, sexy mouth.

'Wouldn't you like to know?' Kimmie smiled as she dipped her head over her work. 'One thing is certain. My drawing will uncover the real you.'

'Should I be worried?'

'Almost certainly,' she murmured.

'I'm eager to see your interpretation,' Kris said dryly.

She pulled a wry grimace. 'As is the rest of the world, I hope.'

This at least was her strength. As soon as her fingers had closed around the familiar pencil, she knew what she was doing, and was confident that the seemingly stark lines on paper would eventually amount to so much more. Relationships were much the same, she reflected as she became lost in her work and her breathing steadied. Built on tiny bricks of action and consequence, they could founder or flourish, depending on whose hand was guiding the pencil. There'd be no more free drawing in her life, Kimmie determined as she sat back to examine her work so far. She would remain in control. Turning the shocks and disappointment of the past thirty-six hours on their head, this new set of paintings would mark a fresh beginning.

'Don't get the wrong idea,' she added as she paused to check she'd got the angle of Kris's jaw exactly right. Yes. It was every bit as strong, firm and resolute as the lines she had laid down on paper. 'My promise not to sell images of you without your permission stands firm. If you do give the go-ahead, any funds they make will go straight into that scholarship fund I told you about.'

'To help young artists,' he confirmed.

'That's right.' She couldn't quite bring herself to ask Kris to be a sponsor of the scheme. It was just another way of asking him for money, and he must be sick of that. This was a better way. She did the work and with his permission the project would hopefully prosper from the sale.

'Would you like to see how far I've got?' she asked when she was nearly finished.

'Of course.' Kris whistled softly beneath his breath when she turned the sketchpad around for him to see. 'You certainly didn't flatter me.'

'I told you I wouldn't. I'm drawing you as I see you today.'

'Hard and driven,' he murmured. 'With an almost frightening sense of purpose in my eyes...' He frowned. 'And no humour at all?'

She huffed a rueful smile. 'If the cap fits.'

'You don't hold back, do you, Kimmie Lancaster?'

'Caution is boring, in art as in life. And how do I know the occasional flashes of humour I see in your eyes aren't just a front you use to lure your victims in?'

'My *victims*?' Kris queried, pulling his head back to look at her.

'Okay, so maybe that's a bit harsh,' Kimmie conceded, 'but I did warn you that I look beneath the surface to see what's there. Are you sure you wouldn't prefer me to flatter you?'

Kris threw up his hands in mock surrender. 'Do what you like,' he said.

'I'll almost certainly be turning these sketches into full-sized paintings,' she thought it only fair to explain.

'Good,' Kris said. 'I look forward to seeing them.'

Would he ever see them? she wondered. 'They're for a good cause.'

'Wouldn't it be better for you to put the proceeds from the sale into a property for yourself?'

'No,' she said, laughing. 'You're such a businessman.'

'I should hope so.'

'And that's the essential difference between us,' she mused. 'You're practical, I'm impractical.'

'It doesn't hurt anyone to have a business head on their shoulders,' Kris countered, 'and it would be essential now you're becoming a success, I would have thought.'

Yes, she should get a handle on that, Kimmie thought uneasily, remembering how she'd agreed to leave all of that side of things to Mike. 'What else has Kyria Demetriou told you about me?' Because she was the only person here who would have told him about her desire to buy her own house.

'I'm quite capable of conducting my own investigations.'

'I won't even ask,' she said, rolling her eyes.

Kris shrugged. 'I stand by my advice.'

'Even if my paintings of you sold for thousands, it would only buy me the door of a shed in London.' Did that sound as if she was asking him for money? It was complicated, knowing a billionaire. Things she'd joke about with her friends suddenly took on a very different significance. She laughed to change the subject and her mood and, to her relief, Kris laughed with her.

'I'd hoped to be worth more than a shed door,' he admitted.

'Well, there you are. You're not worth much after all. And I'm not much of a businesswoman,' Kimmie admitted. 'I don't even know if I'm still the latest "hot young artist", or if my first exhibition was a fluke and my fifteen minutes of fame are already up. The next show should prove it one way or another… That's if I can find someone to exhibit my work,' she added, frowning.

'Can't you pay someone to exhibit your work?'

'It's usually done by the gallery owner taking a commission on every work sold, but I just don't know if anyone will be interested. Believe it or not, Kris Kaimos, not every problem can be solved with money.'

'But how are you supposed to get by until you have your next show? You told me when we met on the beach that you spent a lot of your available cash on the wedding.'

'The non-wedding,' she reminded him. 'I agree, it does sound a bit silly now, reckless even, but when life has thrown me lemons I like to make a good cocktail with them rather than pull an "I sucked a lemon" face.'

'So you always bounce back,' he said thoughtfully.

'I try to. Sometimes it's harder than others,' she admitted. But she'd keep on trying, again and again, until one day she found that home port and an anchor. 'And don't worry—I still have just enough money left to see me through until my next exhibition.'

'I think you've got a pretty clear idea of where you're heading and how to get there,' Kris observed as she closed the sketch pad and put it to one side. 'Everyone has setbacks. It's how you recover from them that counts and I believe in you. I don't mean that to sound patronising.'

'Accepted,' she said.

'Everyone has to start somewhere, even me,' he teased with a wicked grin that warmed her through.

'Don't get too confident,' she warned, 'or the imp inside me will force me to knock you off that pedestal.'

'I'd like to see you try,' he murmured in a way that had everything to do with extremely agreeable physical tussles and nothing whatsoever to do with knocking him down a peg or two. 'In the meantime,' he added in the same husky tone, 'I suggest we dance.'

There were too many decisions to be made where Kris was concerned, and none of them easy. Once bitten, twice shy had gone out of the window some time ago, although the dreaded rebound threat continued to niggle at her, but that didn't stop her standing up as he walked around the table and moving wordlessly into his arms.

CHAPTER SEVEN

IF HE WANTED TO, he could close the deal tonight. His uncle would be pleased. If Theo Kaimos was here now, he would ask—what was Kris waiting for? Here was the bride in need of a groom, the artist in need of a sponsor. Kris needed a wife to provide an heir for Kaimos Shipping and could fund endless scholarships. If Kimmie made that her price for marrying him, he'd pay it gladly. But he didn't want to take her that way. He didn't want to *take* her at all. He wanted Kimmie to come to him of her own free will.

When he took her in his arms to dance and felt how soft and vulnerable she was beneath the simple cotton dress, he knew that nothing with Kimmie would ever be simple. He wanted things with her he'd never thought about before, like a family of his own and someone to share it with. Was the renowned hard man mellowing, the playboy finally considering settling down? Kimmie was an independent woman with ideas of her own about how to live her life. Could she ever truly fit into his? When and if he married, his wife would have no choice but to fall into line and keep pace with his business agenda. His interests were so vast, and his duty towards the people who depended on him for their livelihoods so vitally important, why was he contemplating marrying a boho bride who marched to such a very different beat?

Kimmie pulled away from him and stared into his face, almost as if she had sensed the track his thoughts were taking. She was so sensitive and they were tuned in to each other so acutely it was uncanny. He pulled her close again and heard her sigh. She knew as well as he did that this dance could be a prequel to sex. Had she come to a decision where that was concerned? His mind once more turned back to the knotty problem of marriage. Surely she could learn to be accepting of privileges he took for granted? Many doors would open for her thanks to the Kaimos name. Money would pour into Kimmie's scholarship fund as the great and good stood in line to win his favour. Whatever else she did or didn't agree to, he believed Kimmie would stick doggedly to her pledge to help other young, disadvantaged artists. Whichever way he looked at it, marriage wasn't such a bad option for either of them. He certainly couldn't see a downside for Kimmie. It would be win-win all the way for her.

The instant Kris's arms closed around her, Kimmie felt like a helium balloon soaring high above the crowd. Every part of her was tuned to him, and she was more aware than she'd ever been that this feeling was unique. No one had ever made her see the world in such sharp focus. Mike had always made her feel as if he was doing her a favour—which he was, she had believed at the time—and she'd been so grateful that his interest had only increased with her growing success. She had tried to show her appreciation in silly ways—a few cartoons for him to hang on the wall of his flat…but he hadn't wanted them. Another time she'd knitted him a tie, using paintbrushes as her needles. 'What were you thinking,' he'd said, 'imagining I'd wear something like this? But I love you,' he'd added absently, glancing at the cheque in his hand for one of her paintings. 'You're such a clever girl…'

'Where are you now?' Kris asked, distracting her out of unwelcome memories.

'You don't want to know,' she said slowly.

'Maybe I do…'

'Okay, I'm reviewing what you might call my gullible, desperate period, to use artistic terminology.'

'And where do you find yourself now?'

'In my frying pan and fire period,' she said flippantly.

He laughed and they danced on.

Under the most unusual circumstances, to be sure, but wasn't this just a holiday romance? Was her judgement any better this time around?

Kris's embrace tightened as if he sensed her troubled mind. She felt so safe in his arms, and even that was a dangerous temptation.

'Have you had enough for now?' he asked.

Unseen, she smiled. Could she start again? It wasn't that easy for anyone.

'Would you like to leave?' he prompted.

'Sorry, I was away in a world of my own some-where.'

'Can I join you?' Kris murmured.

Maybe her pencil had lied this time when she'd drawn that hard, driven man. Right now Kris seemed so tender and sympathetic. And the humour was back in his eyes…his amazing, beautiful, expressive eyes.

Was she really so naïve? A mere one day on from absolute betrayal and she was walking eagerly into something so big and powerful it was more likely to sweep her off her feet and dump her in a drain than transport her safely back to home shores.

He drove her back to the beach house. Seeing the property through Kimmie's eyes was like seeing it for the first time. He relied on agents to find houses for him. Any particular requirements he might have were easily catered for and arranged between one of his PAs and the agency. He'd never had cause to complain before, and neither had anyone else, but Kimmie had clearly thought the place sterile and cold. Could she change it? More importantly, would he let her? Did he want it to be changed? Everything worked. He'd never detected any flaws before.

'I'm going to see it all this time,' she said with an air of expectancy.

'I tremble,' he teased.

'No need to tremble,' she said with a wry shake of her head. 'I'm sure it's still every bit as fabulous as I remember.'

'But too big for one man,' he reminded her.

'Did I say that?' She pressed her lips down, but her eyes were twinkling. 'How rude of me.'

He smiled, and then she glanced away from him as they drove by his private harbour, where a number of different craft were rising and falling in time to the ocean, dark shadows swaying in time to their own music in the moonlight. 'Impressive,' she said.

'Something else you'd like to paint?' he guessed.

'I'm not sure I'll be here long enough to record everything.' She paused and turned to look at him. 'I want to get you down on paper first.'

'That has to be the first time a woman has ever said that to me,' he confessed.

'I don't want to hear about your other women,' she reprimanded.

'I'm duly rebuked. But don't you have enough sketches of me by now?'

'Not from every angle, dressed and undressed,' she admitted with complete frankness.

'Undressed?' he exclaimed, taken aback.

'Why not?' she said candidly. 'Life classes were my favourite at college. They say you can judge a book by its cover, but I prefer to remove the dust jacket and get right down to brass tacks.'

'You might find a lot more than you expected.'

'I'll take my chances on that, though understand this, Kris Kaimos,' she said with a direct look that made him raise an eyebrow. 'I might be inexperienced when it comes to romance but, as an artist, when it comes to the male form I've already seen everything.'

'Fair enough,' he said, choosing not to disagree.

'Last chance for me to take you back to the guest house,' he warned as they approached the turning, 'so if you'd rather leave my unveiling for another day, you'd better say now.'

She shot him a glance. 'Do you want to take me back?'

'I want to swim,' he said honestly. Most of all, he didn't want to rush this.

'You want to swim?' she queried with a disbelieving frown.

'I need to cool down. Something wrong with that?'

'Nothing, but I thought you were taking me to see the artist's studio?'

'Afterwards,' he said. 'I promise there'll be time for everything.'

'Thanks. As a professional observer, it's important for me to see where people live, and how they live. The more I learn about you, the more layered your portrait will be.'

'Oh, forget about that for now. Just paint me while I'm swimming in the water. That will tell you all you need to know.'

'Power and drive, and getting where you want to go at high speed and as straight as an arrow?' she suggested.

'It doesn't always work out like that.' Not with Kimmie, certainly. 'Why don't you join me for a swim?'

'I don't have a costume.'

'Neither do I,' he pointed out.

'Kris Kaimos,' she said, acting shocked. 'What are you suggesting?'

'One of those life classes you mentioned.'

That kept her quiet, and she said nothing more until they reached the side of the pool. The lighting scheme here was genius. It meant she could see clearly, swim naked, and still feel cloaked to some extent in shadow.

'You're a very lucky man,' she remarked in a tone that suggested to him that she was already sketching the scene in her mind. 'Do you mind me painting some scenes from here when I get home?' she asked. 'I mean, if you'd rather keep your home life private, I totally understand.'

'Generally, I do like to keep it private,' he admitted, 'but scenes in isolation could be located anywhere in the world. Surely it's up to the artist to convey the mood and purpose of a subject, without necessarily revealing its location.'

'You really get this, don't you?' she mused.

'I get you,' he countered.

'You think you do,' she corrected him quietly.

'Meaning?'

She stared at him for a few intense moments which left him utterly convinced that what he needed was a challenge like Kimmie Lancaster in his life, and maybe she needed him just as badly in hers.

'I'm starting to know you,' he amended. 'Others

might sell their paintings for personal gain, but not you. In fact, I wish you would.'

'You can't change me.'

'I wouldn't want to.'

'If my paintings of you and of Kaimos do sell well, it's also to my advantage,' she pointed out frankly. 'The publicity would be incredible.'

'And you deserve that sort of break.'

'How do you know?' she asked. 'Maybe you should wait and see what I come up with before you say things like that. It might be rubbish,' she fired back.

'I doubt that somehow. Though it does mean we'd have to see each other again,' he said, acting as if this was a problem.

'Not necessarily,' she argued, calling his bluff. 'You can visit an exhibition without meeting the artist.'

A timely reminder that Kimmie was her own woman—always had been, always would be—and in all honesty he couldn't blame her. She'd somehow scrambled out of a troubled childhood relatively un-scathed, and then she'd tried to ally herself to a man who'd proved totally unworthy of her. It was no won-der that art was her rock now. 'Do you have a venue in mind for the exhibition?'

'Not exactly,' she admitted, 'but I'll find some-where, even if it's a village hall. The swish Lon-don gallery that hosted my last exhibition is usually booked out months in advance. The owners might not consider my next collection, as their preference is for drama and darkness, which was why my childhood retrospective held such strong appeal for them. I created the body of work for my finals at college, never expecting I would sell it to the public, but it's customary for gallery owners to view the work of students who are leaving college, and I was lucky enough to be taken up.'

'You say it was dark?' he queried, remembering with a frown what she'd told him of her early life.

'Pretty grim, to be honest,' she admitted, 'though I think working on it was actually healing for me. I managed to visit all the dark corners in my mind and lay them down on canvas, in the light, for all to see, where they couldn't do any more harm. I guess lots of people could relate to that, because they sold out right away. Now I'm going to turn from the dark side to making people smile, but that might not go down so well commercially.'

'You won't know until you try,' he commented.

'True,' she said, 'and I'm determined that my next collection will zing with sunshine and happiness so everyone leaves smiling. Life's hard enough without always hanging the dark side on the wall.' She shrugged and grinned. 'We'll just have to see how this change of direction goes down.'

'Time for that swim,' he announced. The more he learned about Kimmie, the more he wanted her, so much so that right now he badly needed cold water and plenty of it.

Kris's expression was hidden in shadow. It was so easy talking to him. Too easy, maybe. A man as successful as Kristof Kaimos was hardly likely to be uncomplicated, so why was he devoting so much time to a fledgling artist without a penny to her name and certainly no social standing? Did he have an agenda? If so, what was it? And did things need to go any deeper between them? Couldn't she just enjoy tonight?

'Swim first, explore later,' she confirmed. Why not?

Maybe because Kris's thumb was already lodged in the back of his top and, as he dragged it over his head, the sight of his naked torso made her heart thunder.

'Your turn,' he prompted, shucking off his jeans.

Her limbs were glued in place. Even if she'd still been holding her sketchbook, she doubted she would have the ability to record such perfection.

'Something wrong?' he asked casually.

Did he really not know? Kris clearly had no inhibitions.

Would you with a body like that?

Might look a bit odd on me, but…

'You're laughing?' he asked, a hint of outrage in his tone.

'Not at you. Just at the thought of me getting naked and standing next to you.'

'We're not posing for a painting. There won't be much standing around.'

'Yes, but you seem to find it really easy…doing the Michelangelo thing, I mean…and I'm just not sure I will.'

'You wear underwear, don't you?'

'None of your business,' she warned.

'It will be soon,' Kris pointed out, grinning.

She swallowed hard as his teeth flashed white in the moonlight. Oh, what the heck? Her underwear was nothing if not respectable. Some might even call it boring. There was a lot to be said for underwear bought in packs of three. It was certainly more concealing than her bikini. Now all she had to do was keep her own gaze under control, and remember not to look at Kris below his non-existent belt.

'Are you recording the specifics for later consideration?' he suggested wickedly when she failed miserably to keep her pledge even as she whipped off her dress.

'It's important to get the detail right,' she insisted, tongue firmly lodged in her cheek, while her heart beat at the speed of a hummingbird's wings as she asked herself for the umpteenth time since meeting Kris: *What was she doing here?*

'Of course it is,' Kris agreed in the same teasing tone.

'Or I could just go for direct action,' she threatened. Launching herself at him, she tried to take him down. The pool was just behind him.

Kris didn't move.

She had badly misjudged her target.

'Playing games, are we?' He advanced one silent step at a time.

'No,' she warned, holding up her hands as she backed away. 'I like to get into the pool slowly.'

'This isn't your lucky day then, is it?'

She screamed as they hit the pool in tandem.

Things happened so fast after that. Kris's strong arms were wrapped around her. He was in his depth. She was not. Supporting her in the water, he drove his mouth down on hers.

Yes...yes...yes!

Whatever had happened up to this moment, nothing had ever felt like this. The combination of cold and heat, hard and soft sharpened Kimmie's awareness to an almost painful degree. The salt of the water and Kris's minty fresh taste pummelled her senses and so did his hands as they held and supported, touched and caressed. The way he made her feel, everything about him, about this, came together and made sense. Winding her arms around his neck and her legs around his waist seemed the next obvious move and, before she knew it, she was kissing him back.

CHAPTER EIGHT

WHEN HE RAISED his head she was breathless. 'Don't ever do that again,' she gasped. 'I don't swim as well as you.'

'No more kisses,' Kris agreed.

'That's not what I meant and you know it.'

He smiled. Deliciously wet and wickedly handsome, he now declared, 'I don't know what you're worried about. I'll always save you.'

'I don't need saving.'

'Don't you?' he whispered. And then he kissed her again, proving her wrong.

She certainly didn't want to be saved from this situation. After a lifetime of fearing sex because of her mother's experience at her father's hands, she felt—no, she knew with utter certainty—that it would be different with Kris. She wanted this incredible night to remember for ever. A feeling had lodged deep inside her that said it would heal her, pleasure her and allow her to know, however briefly, how it felt to be close to someone, to be one with them and to trust again. Closing her eyes, she rejoiced in the strength and beauty of Kris's body. Enfolded in his arms, she felt so safe. This might be an illusion that only lasted one night but while she had it she'd hold on tight.

'Hussy,' Kris mock scolded as she rubbed herself shamelessly against his body. She'd never been so bold before, but her usual behaviour had flown out of the window. 'You feel amazing over these prim little pants,' he observed as she groaned openly with pleasure. 'Plump, warm and inviting,' he commented in a matter-of-fact tone. She was certainly incapable of speech. 'Nice?' he murmured as he caressed her again.

Was he seriously asking that question? Kris could have no idea how good it felt. Mapping her contours over her suddenly thrillingly inadequate pants, he really did have the most intuitive touch.

'You have no idea,' she whispered hoarsely.

'I think I do,' he argued in a husky tone as streams of honeyed desire surged through her veins.

Encouraging her to relax the grip of her legs around his waist, he held her in the water so she was floating. Allowing her thighs to part a little allowed more intimate touches, she discovered. Being pleasured so skilfully soon had her teetering on the edge. She'd waited so long for this she couldn't wait any longer. Her body was his to command.

'Are you sure?' he asked as he thrilled her neck with seductive open-mouthed kisses.

'Do I have a choice?'

'Always,' he said firmly.

'Then I choose this,' she said, reaching for her underwear.

Kris took over, removing what remained with skilful ease and then, still supporting her in the water, he dipped his head and kissed her again.

'More?' he suggested.

'Oh, yes please…'

Every part of her was aroused, and as he massaged her breasts with his free hand her nipples grew taut and erect. But that wasn't nearly enough for her and, opening her legs just a little bit more, she invited him to take advantage.

'Relax,' he said. 'I've got you, *agape mou*.'

Supporting her on his arm, Kris's encouragement in his own language really turned her on. Her body obliged him, and her thighs parted even more.

'That's good,' he approved as she spread her legs wide. 'That's perfect. But I think you need careful preparation before I go any further.'

'Oh, yes, I do,' she agreed as Kris began to touch her intimately, but with the utmost delicacy and sensitivity that gave her absolutely no reason to fear him. 'How do you know exactly what I need?' she asked somehow on a shaking breath.

'All sorts of clues,' he murmured as he began to circle her most sensitive core. 'You flinched when I first touched you, for example.'

'You're reading a lot into that,' Kimmie remarked, frowning.

'My intuition again,' Kris said as he arranged her to his liking.

'Ah…don't stop,' she whimpered as his finger-tips drew ever closer to where she needed him to be. Whatever she'd felt in the past, Kris had the an-swer as he mapped each of her deliciously arousal-swollen curves.

'Are you a virgin?' he pressed as she groaned with pleasure.

'Do you care?' she panted as he increased the pressure very slightly.

'Of course I care. And of course it matters. Does it put me off? What do you think?' he asked as he kissed her deeply, slowly.

'Have mercy on me,' she pleaded when he lifted his head. 'You can't keep teasing me like this.'

'Yes, I can,' he assured her.

He smiled down at her in the moonlight. With the swish of the water and Kimmie's soft moans the only sounds to be heard as he pleasured her, this was turn-ing into the most romantic seduction. He couldn't re-member ever feeling like this before, or smiling so often. He wanted to do far more than please Kim-mie; he wanted to reassure her and make her feel safe. A measure of this was that he had never been in so much frustrated pain in his life, but he would do nothing to startle Kimmie or rush this just to sat-isfy himself, because she deserved the most sensitive awakening he could give her.

'Please,' she begged, losing all inhibitions now. 'Kiss me again, touch me again… *Ahh…*'

Kisses that were tender became driven by mu-tual fire until she was trembling on the point of release. 'More!' she commanded fiercely. 'Unless you don't want to?'

'Don't want to?' he queried incredulously. Of course I do.' For a moment he stared at her, uncomprehending, and then he realised that it must be those whispers from childhood still plaguing her. He knew only too well how they could become shouts at times. 'I want you,' he stated with absolute conviction.

'And I want you,' she gasped.

'Like this?' he murmured as he held her safe and used his free hand to increase the sensations.

'Exactly like that,' she exclaimed.

'I won't rush this,' he warned her as he purposefully slowed the tempo again.

'Why not?' she demanded and, taking matters into her own hands, she ground her body against his fist until release was no longer a distant prospect but a howling, screaming reality. 'Take me here in the water,' she begged the moment the powerful release had begun to ease off.

'Certainly not,' he told her, smiling against her mouth as he kissed her. 'This is going to take a lot of time and a considerable amount of pleasure before we reach that point, so you will have to be patient.'

'And if I won't be?'

'Then I shall punish you.'

'Please,' she breathed, her eyes bright with excitement.

'By withholding pleasure,' he explained.

'Don't you dare!'

He enjoyed seeing her still moving rhythmically

in time to the fading pulses. 'I think you want more,' he murmured.

'You only think that? Anyway,' she assured him, 'I'm not thinking at all.'

Dipping his head, he brushed her mouth with his lips. As he did so, her legs floated to the surface of the water and parted. His hand found her, and this time she covered his hand with hers, showing him exactly what she needed, and how fast she needed it. He gave it to her efficiently, satisfying her as quickly as she wanted. Then, kissing her again, he plundered her mouth with his tongue and her body with his fingers, all the time murmuring words of reassurance and encouragement in his own language until she was completely lost to pleasure. Gasping rhythmically with approval, she whimpered in time to her growing need and he responded the way she wanted, watching through half-closed eyes as she approached the edge again and prepared to fall over.

'And now I'm going to make you wait,' he announced.

'No!' she wailed.

'Then you must tell me what you want this time,' he insisted.

'I want you… I want this. I want you deep inside me,' she gasped out.

'You want everything, in fact,' he confirmed.

'Yes!'

Kris was all she needed to forget the past and start building her life again. This was so much more than sex. It was salvation. Breath caught in her throat as he lifted her out of the water and held her against him. Then he turned her so her back was pressed hard against his torso. Her pulse spiked with excitement as he cupped her breasts, holding her above the water.

'Good?' he asked as he kissed her neck, sending streams of sensation streaking through her. 'What about this?' One hand moved steadily lower until he found her. She was still frustrated and slick with need. He hummed appreciatively as he discovered this, but she made no sound. She didn't dare to break the spell. Her senses were floating like her body, out of reach and beyond her control.

'Please…don't make me wait.'

He knew exactly what she needed and laughed softly as he instructed, 'When I say you can, and not before.'

She went absolutely still as he began to work. She knew what to expect now, and how good it would be. 'You need this,' he murmured as he applied a little more pressure.

'Yes, I do,' she agreed heatedly. She could only marvel at the possibilities for ecstasy contained within her body that she hadn't even known about. 'Now!' she begged.

'No,' he murmured and to make sure of it he withdrew his hand. 'When I say and not before.'

'Oh, please…' She was teetering above the abyss, longing to plunge into it again.

'Don't rush,' he counselled in the calmest of

tones. 'If you wait until I say, the feeling will be even greater.'

Believing him, she forced her mind somewhere else. But she couldn't hold on. Her body wouldn't allow her to. Kris hadn't just applied more pressure, he'd speeded up. 'I can't!' she cried out as his knowing hand continued to move to a steady and reliable rhythm.

'You must wait,' he said evenly. 'I will tell you when you can let go.'

'No!' she wailed.

'Yes,' he insisted in a tone of command.

'I really can't,' she protested in a whimper.

'Then, I'll stop,' he threatened.

'I hate you!'

'No, you don't,' he said confidently.

Grinding her jaw, she held her breath and closed her eyes until the urge to leap into the alluring black velvet depths had subsided once again.

'Good,' Kris praised. 'Now you shall have your reward.'

He made sure of it, and when the storm broke she screamed on and on because the reward for waiting was just as he'd said. Cataclysmic waves of sensation dashed all rational thought from her brain. She might have yelled so loudly her friends back in the village could hear her. She certainly groaned repeatedly in time to each delicious pulse. With no idea of the sounds she was making, she couldn't have cared less. Reduced to primal need and nothing more, she hardly knew her own name, let alone anything else, and when clear thinking finally did return it was accompanied by one thing, and that was the urgent need for more.

The rush of triumph he felt at finally finding a woman who could match him where passion was concerned had made him doubly hard, but it was Kimmie's unique mix of sexual hunger and relative innocence that touched him the most. She had made him feel again, care again, and that had never happened before. Sex had always been a good physical workout in the past, but it had left him feeling empty and, although they had yet to consummate their relationship, he knew it wouldn't be like that with Kimmie. But he didn't care about personal physical satisfaction, only that she should know the best and be happy. There was more to come, there was everything to come, so why rush a single second of it?

When he finally lowered her to her feet in the pool, he made sure she was hanging on to the side while he sprang out to grab some towels. 'Here,' he said, helping her out and wrapping her up warmly. 'We'll take a hot shower in the house.'

'And then complete the tour?' she said shakily.

'If your legs will hold you up,' he teased.

'If they don't it's your fault,' she said with a tremulous smile.

He watched as she began to wrap herself up like an Egyptian mummy in a number of towels. 'Don't do that,' he whispered. Unpeeling one of the towelling bandages from around her collarbone, he kissed that tender spot and then her neck. 'You're beautiful,' he whispered, 'and you've done absolutely nothing wrong.'

'Beautiful?' she queried in that semi-comic way Kimmie adopted when she was feeling insecure. 'And as for doing nothing wrong?' she exclaimed, pulling a face.

He dragged her close to kiss her as her face twisted in a fretting expression. Anger filled him. He wanted to find the people who'd hurt her and make them beg for Kimmie's forgiveness. He had never met a woman as strong and yet as vulnerable as she was. Kimmie's spirit spoke to him in ways he couldn't explain. She filled him with the urge to be her dragon-slayer, and the irony was she didn't need anyone to do that for her. Kimmie was quite capable of handling life by herself.

'You're beautiful,' he repeated, holding her at arm's length so he could stare intently into her eyes.

'Thank you,' she whispered.

He hoped she believed him.

She looked around with interest when he took her into the house. And then she turned back to him with a worried look on her face. 'Would you be angry if I said I used you to forget?'

'Did you?'

She was silent for quite a while and then admitted quietly, 'Even I don't know.'

'Do you hear me complaining?'

There was another silence and then she said, 'Do you always make people feel this good?'

'Not always,' he admitted truthfully.

'I'm looking forward to that shower,' she said, shivering slightly, 'and then the tour of the house.'

His plans lay in quite a different direction. *From jilted bride to cherished bride* crossed his mind as he lifted Kimmie to carry her into the house. There wasn't much wrong with that, and it was becoming increasingly likely. Life had taught him never to ignore a seemingly random act of fate. He had yet to learn the ins and outs of her career, but they were both slaves to duty, that much he knew, so there was a strong chance she'd understand if he was away most of the time. It went without saying she'd have the best help available. Professional nannies, if and when necessary, and accommodation of her choice. These were things he could deliver. Another option was for Kimmie to build or buy a property to her own taste. He didn't foresee any problems going forward.

CHAPTER NINE

HAVING SWEPT HER into his arms, Kris carried her up the stairs as if she weighed nothing. 'We're dripping all over the house,' she pointed out, laughing a little with sheer excitement.

'Who's going to tell us off?'

Now they were both laughing as he jogged up the stairs. She had never felt freer in her life, or more un-inhibited. As they mounted the impressive staircase she got the briefest glimpse of white, taupe and ivory décor, punctuated by vivid splashes of modern art. She had no doubt they were genuine, but the detail was lost on her because she was lost in Kris's eyes.

At the top of the stairs polished wood gave way to plush cream carpet that ate up every sound as Kris took them down a broad corridor. Subtly lit so that it glowed invitingly in shades of amber and peach, Kimmie guessed they'd reached the sleeping quarters, though chances were there'd be more than sleeping happening here tonight.

'Thoughts?' he prompted, feeling her tense in his arms.

'You must have great staff to keep a place like this so pristine,' she said, avoiding riskier topics now the moment of no turning back had arrived.

'Changed your mind?' he asked softly, reading her shrewdly as always.

'No,' she said firmly. Whatever life held in the future, she needed this, needed Kris, even if it was for just one night. She'd made her decision and no way was she going back on it now.

With a nod of acknowledgement, Kris shouldered the door and it swung open on silent hinges to reveal a large, tastefully decorated room. Free from clutter, his bedroom boasted another superb lighting scheme, which he turned down until it was only a glimmer. The only way the room fell short was on the cosy front. For all its opulence, expensive tech and design features, it was more like a top-end hotel room, kept ready for its VIP guest, rather than a sanctuary to block out the rattle of the day. Kimmie guessed anything Kris owned would be the same. Kept up to the mark by an army of staff so he could land anywhere at any time and be sure of the same impersonal yet dependable welcome. Her last thought as he laid her down on the bed was that there was nothing to envy here. If Kris's house had failings, he had none, she thought as he shed his towel and stood naked in front of her. How she wanted him. But…

No buts. Stop thinking too hard. Or she'd think herself straight out of this and then she'd have the rest of her life to regret not going through with it. Yet, despite her own mental urgings, what might be in it for Kris couldn't help but cross her mind.

'What about the shower and tour?' she asked as he joined her on the bed.

'I like you damp and tasting of salt.'

A nagging doubt was stubbornly ticking over in her mind. 'Is this pure passion for you, or do you have an agenda?'

'What?' Kris pulled back his head to stare down at her.

'Perhaps I'm just another notch on your bedpost?' she suggested.

'Please,' he said, drawing her into his arms. 'You have an overactive imagination, and a very suspicious mind.'

'Kyria Demetriou would say I'm too trusting.'

'And Kyria Demetriou is always right.'

'Yes,' Kimmie murmured thoughtfully. If her elderly friend trusted Kris, should she do the same?

'What did she tell you about me?' Kris asked.

'Not to trust you,' she lied, giving him a wink. 'Actually, every time Kyria Demetriou mentioned you it was to praise you to the skies.'

As Kris laughed and relaxed, she went one step further. 'Then again, she would like me to believe that not all men are bad.'

'And you think they are?' Kris growled softly as he stretched like a panther to make himself comfortable on the bed.

Turning onto her back, Kimmie stared up at the ceiling. 'Do you know what I'd really like now?'

When Kris remained silent, she said, 'I'd like a hug.' Turning her face, she looked him in the eyes. 'Sometimes that's all you need, you know?'

Reaching across the bed, he drew her into his arms and held her in an unthreatening way, which prompted her to admit that Kyria Demetriou had also urged her to try again where men were concerned, and that her experience with Mike shouldn't sour her for life.

'And here you are with me, which is far from ideal,' Kris commented, 'For you, that is,' he clarified. 'I'm quite happy.'

'Are you?' Kimmie asked softly. 'Anyway, now you know everything.'

'I very much doubt that,' Kris argued gently in between dropping kisses on the top of her head.

'I'll take my chances,' she said.

He could only marvel at how tiny and vulnerable she was. 'Don't cover yourself,' he said as she crossed her arms over her chest on top of the legion of towels. 'You should be proud of how you look.'

Her answer to this was to cross her legs and turn slightly on to her side. 'I'm not—'

'You are,' he insisted. 'You're beautiful.'

'And you're always right?'

'Invariably,' he confirmed, teasing her with a smile and more kisses.

'Why me?'

'Why not you?' he countered, frowning.

'Is this to your advantage somehow?'

'What a thing to say.'

'Is it?' Kimmie probed, her forehead pleating. 'I know how driven you are, and I think you'd do pretty much anything to get—'

He kissed the next words out of her mouth. The stinging accuracy with which she intuited at least part of his motivation for tonight had shocked him, and it didn't make him feel very good about himself. 'Why are you so suspicious?'

'Life made me that way, and things are happening so fast between us.'

'Because we both want them to.'

'True,' she agreed. 'But I'm hardly the most attractive woman in my group of friends, so why pick me?'

'Who can account for attraction?' he said with an evasive shrug, guessing this was all about a gentle lead up to the inevitable.

'So you're not another gold-digger with profit in mind when I become a world-famous artist?' she teased with a cheeky look.

He laughed out loud and she laughed with him. 'You've certainly got a talent for turning things on their head. I know you're joking, but let me reassure you that you're by far the most fascinating as well as the most beautiful woman I've ever met, and your delaying tactics are second to none.'

'Is it that obvious?'

'Yes.'

'So…?'

'So, I've told you before, I like a challenge.'

'So do I,' she assured him gently.

The frown had faded from her face but there were still questions in her eyes he didn't want to answer. Beneath her outwardly confident exterior Kimmie still felt crushed and shamed by the wedding fiasco, and was so ready to be hurt again he wished he'd never spoken to his uncle, had never considered getting married just to please Theo, and had certainly avoided throwing Kimmie into the ring as a contender. How could she be certain of him when they hardly knew each other? And yet he felt the stirrings of something for her that was out of the ordinary. If she ever found out that he had even half an eye on searching for a suitable bride, she'd be devastated.

'Kiss me,' she whispered, distracting him.

His troubling thoughts stood no chance against a sensual onslaught by Kimmie. He wanted to know this woman in every way there was and when their lips touched and he plundered her mouth he knew it would only be a short time before he claimed her completely.

Kris unpeeled each of the towels in turn until she lay beneath him, completely naked.

'No,' he warned when she automatically moved to cross her arms over her chest again. Taking hold of both her wrists in one big hand, he pinned them lightly above her head. Then, slipping one muscular thigh between her legs, he parted them just a little… just enough.

'You really want this?' he murmured, making absolutely sure she was with him every step of the way.

'Yes,' she breathed.

Dropping kisses on her body until she relaxed, he moved down the bed, making everywhere he touched quiver with pleasure. Stroking and soothing, he finally dipped his head to give her the most intimate kiss of all. She tensed with a gasp, having never experienced anything so sexually adventurous. The level of intimacy was shocking at first, but it flung her into a new world where anything and everything was possible if it made her feel like this. Her gasp soon softened into a series of rhythmic moans as her body undulated in time to the laving of Kris's tongue. He knew exactly what to do and how to prolong her enjoyment…when to hold back and when to start again. He didn't need to tell her to relax. She was fully engaged and responsive. The hunt for release was an all-consuming passion, her only goal.

'Yes, now,' she gritted out and, unlike before, he didn't make her wait.

She screamed wildly and repeatedly as she claimed her reward, and then groaned contentedly as the crashing waves of intense pleasure gradually subsided into pleasurable little clenches. 'Good…*so good*,' she managed as he started again.

But this time he left her hanging right on the edge. 'No…don't stop!'

Nothing she could say would move him to rush. Protecting them both, he moved to kneel between her legs and fisted his erection. Her throat dried at the sight of Kris's massive hand barely able to enclose it. She'd never been this close to so much man before, had never inhaled such a potent mix of heat and sex. Kris was powerful, sex incarnate, and all the more desirable in her eyes for being so dark and rugged against her fragile skin. He hadn't shaved recently and his stubble was thick and black and sharp. His wild hair had dried and the tiny gold hoop in his ear glinted in its depths. Tattoos on his upper arms pointed up the size of his biceps, while his chest was broad and strong. Everything about him excited her. He was the personification of danger and she was aroused by his brutal, swarthy good looks. She wanted him, and had no intention of waiting this time. Bending her legs, she spread them and, cupping each thigh, she held them apart. She had to have this…him, before she returned home. She was hungry for the touch of a man who knew what he was doing in the bedroom before she resigned herself to mediocrity again.

Kris refused to be hurried and nothing she could do would change his mind. The fact that he stared down, taking note of her readiness, and then did nothing to hurry things on, only aroused her more. Smoothing the hair back from her face with his free hand, he dipped his head and kissed her. It was as if he had to make one last check that she was up for this. His breathing was the only thing that gave him away. It was a little heavier now. But it was nowhere near as hectic as hers, Kimmie realised when she paused to listen. Everything about Kris was on a grand scale, while she had never felt smaller when he brushed just the tip of his erection against her.

'Please,' she heard herself beg. 'Don't make me wait. I need you now. *Please…*'

'You're not frightened?'

'No!'

Kris's answer was to brush himself repeatedly against her. It was the most incredible feeling, like everything he'd done to her before, only ten times more effective. When he allowed just the tip of his erection to catch inside her, she stilled, buoyant on a wave of pleasure but afraid to move in case he took it as a signal to take her roughly. Nothing could be further from the truth. Kris was measured and completely in control to the point where she groaned with disappointment when he withdrew and whimpered excitedly when he allowed himself to penetrate just a little way inside her. Her nipples were so tight they hurt and her breasts had never felt heavier, while between her legs had become a swollen, greedy place. Air hissed between her teeth as he inserted the smooth, rounded tip again, and this time she was rewarded with a little more pressure as he began to stretch her.

'Oh, no,' she cried as he pulled out again. *'Please…'*

Reaching beneath her, he cupped her buttocks to raise them even higher off the bed. Her world was composed entirely of sensation. She didn't care what he did. And then he leaned forward and very slowly took her to the hilt. She cried out at his invasion and bit hard into the muscular flesh of his shoulder. He tasted of heat and sex and sunshine, and hot, clean man. And she growled as she held herself open, inviting more. Having positioned her for maximum pleasure, Kris allowed her to get used to the sensation of being completely filled by him before moving slowly to withdraw. The loss of him was such a shock she cried out again, but he didn't make her wait long before taking her again. Inserting himself carefully, he sank deep and then repeated the steady move several times more, which quickly brought her to the edge. This time when she said 'Please,' all it took was several firm thrusts to make her lose control and, as she did so, Kris remained deep inside her where he could massage her to the finish. Writhing helplessly beneath him as the orgasm gradually faded, she could only ask for more.

'Much more?' he suggested with a raised eyebrow.

'Oh, yes, I think so,' she gasped.

Floating on some higher level of awareness, she was content to obey him for once, when Kris said he would do all the work and she must lie still and concentrate on sensation. 'Nothing more, just that,' he urged.

She'd do so happily, and had no complaint as he efficiently brought her to the edge again. 'Now,' he commanded softly, and she did exactly as he instructed.

An hour or so later, confident she was used to him after about her fourth cataclysmic release, Kris turned her so he was kneeling behind her on the bed.

'Raise your hips,' he murmured, 'so I can touch you while I take you.'

Resting her head on her forearms, she lifted her

hips as high as she could, and was instantly rewarded by the sensation of Kris's big hands holding her in position as he filled her and touched her all at the same time.

He wasn't so gentle now, and he pounded into her as she commanded him to work faster… *'Harder…! Now…! Please now!'* Her loss of control was noisy and wild, but Kris's hands were firm on her buttocks to keep her in place so she could enjoy every last pulse of pleasure. Wailing, she thrashed about, but his grip was firm, giving her no alternative but to take everything he had to give her. Bucking helplessly in the throes of an orgasm so extreme she doubted either of them could survive it, she finally slumped on to the bed while Kris worked some magic with his hand to make sure she was quite finished.

'More?' he queried when she was finally quiet.

'Stop teasing me… Let me catch my breath. Don't you need a rest?' she demanded groggily. Turning her head, she smiled a secret smile. 'Obviously not,' she murmured contentedly.

Moving behind her, Kris proved her right. Wrapping his body around hers until they were like spoons, he rested her leg on top of his and, having spread her wide, he took her again.

CHAPTER TEN

Now SHE WAS over her fear of sex, intimacy with Kimmie was wilder and more fun than he could ever have anticipated. And intensely pleasurable too.

Far from tiring of each other, let alone getting tired, it seemed the more they had, the more they wanted from each other. She was demanding. He was too. Even now, with her back turned to him, she had curled up in a ball, raising her buttocks as high as she could to tease and tempt him into delivering more prolonged and diligent attention. She was so tight and hot, and so surprisingly inventive. Far from the ingénue he'd first thought her, Kimmie Lancaster was an extremely sexy woman who'd been trapped in a shell of inexperience and lack of opportunity.

Lack of opportunity?

The thought of her being with another man hit him like a freight train, and it did not feel good. He could not, would not allow that to happen.

As she reached the edge of the plateau of pleasure where he'd been keeping her with steady, reliable strokes, she reached behind her to grab hold of whatever she could. Her fingers were like steel as she urged him on. He'd be covered in battle scars by the morning, and would relish every one.

'Now,' she commanded with all the confidence she'd gained over the past few hours.

Bucking furiously as the waves of her release lashed her into a frenzy, she tightened her inner muscles around him, which made holding back an impossibility. His release was extraordinary. Powerful, and seemingly never-ending, he had never known anything like it before. When they had both finally quietened, he embraced her and she wrapped her arms around him as they laughed and kissed and gasped with sheer disbelief that anything could feel quite so good.

'And now I'm going to ride you,' she said.

'Mercy!'

'There can be no mercy for a man who has so much potential.'

'Okay, then.' He shrugged and turned onto his back.

'But first…' Moving down the bed, she took him in her mouth and made him harder still. 'That's better,' she approved.

He helped her mount up, and from there it was a crazy ride to the finish.

'Amazing,' she gasped. 'You're amazing!'

'And you are too,' he confirmed, smiling.

Turning her, he slipped a pillow beneath her hips to lift her into an even more receptive position. As he did so, she met his gaze and held it. 'I love this,' she said as his rough hands cupped her buttocks.

'You do surprise me,' he said wryly.

As they laughed together, intimately sharing their own particular brand of humour, he realised that sex had never been fun before. It had been a means to an end, a hunger satisfied, a need dealt with until the next time, but this…*this* was something very different.

Never in her wildest dreams had Kimmie imagined that sex could be as good as this. Not just good—fantastic. Or that she could feel the way she did about Kris. He wasn't just the consummate lover; he made her feel loved, cherished…special. She didn't expect the feeling to last. They were worlds apart and she had to be realistic, but while they were here making memories that would have to be enough. She'd treasure those memories, and believed absolutely that they would make her artwork richer and more layered in so many ways. How could she portray life and love without ever experiencing these feelings?

It was late the next day while Kimmie was in the shower that he decided to definitely etch her name right at the top of his so far non-existent list of potential brides. They'd only known each other a few days, but how long would it take to know that this was different and special? The sex was amazing. She made him laugh, made him relax, made him look at life differently. That definitely put her in contention.

She would be leaving Kaimos soon. He wasn't sure of the exact date. He'd been too busy, to put it mildly, to ask questions he'd thought could wait.

Rolling over in bed to answer the phone, he fielded a call from one of his PAs in New York. Instantly alert at hearing some disastrous news, he was already making plans to leave the island. Not tomorrow, unfortunately, but right now. The crucially important deal he'd thought he'd sewn up had sprung a leak that only his finger could plug. Quitting the rumpled bed, he strode into the bathroom and joined Kimmie beneath the spray.

'Again?' she whispered as she wrapped her arms around his neck and stared up, smiling.

'Why not?' he agreed, backing her towards the wall. They didn't have long, but it was enough.

Would he ever get enough of this woman? He knew the answer even as he lifted her and she wrapped her legs around his waist. Pressing her up against cool marble, he took her with crazy passion, and with frustration that they didn't have longer to spin this out. He could hardly propose they saw each other again just so he could assess her suitability as a potential bride some time in the future. It would be better to walk away now.

But what would that say to Kimmie? *Yeah, the sex was great, but I can't have you interfering with my life.*

Wasn't that actually what he was saying, and how it would be if he went ahead with his crazy plan?

'I've never known anyone like you,' he whispered in her ear as the screaming died down and soft, rhythmical moans took its place. 'You do know how special you are to me, don't you?'

With a deep sigh, she stared up, holding his gaze with an expression that took hold of his heart and twisted it. 'Are? Or have been?' she said with her usual intuitive shrewdness. 'Don't make any promises to me that you can't keep, Kris. I couldn't take that.'

'I'm not going to,' he assured her, trying to close down his feelings. 'I have to go away,' he admitted. 'Right now. Business. But I'll be back, and I still want to see that exhibition. If that's all right with you?'

She blinked rapidly and drew a deep breath. 'If I'm not too busy, I might make time for you,' she said, though her teasing sounded strained. 'You know us artists,' she continued. 'We get lost in our own world and forget about everything else. So there's a big chance I might forget about you too.'

'Paint me and remember,' he said, selfishly hoping she would.

'And now you have to go,' she reminded him lightly.

'Yes. Do you mind if I rush?' he asked, grimacing. 'I have a flight plan to file and arrangements to make.'

'You go,' she reiterated. 'I'll be fine.'

Kimmie had never seen anyone dress so quickly, or leave a situation so fast. There was a life lesson right there. Mike had never loved her, she realised now, and yet she'd fallen for the combination of his familiarity and charm. Kris had exploded into her life, changing everything, but had rocketed out of it just as fast. The thought of him leaving so rapidly after what had been such a special moment for her—for both of them, she'd thought—had left her with an aching heart and a sinking feeling in her stomach that she had never been in control, as she'd imagined, and that she had to get a grip before she slid down the cracks opening up in every direction.

Sitting down heavily on the bed, she threw her head back to stare at the ceiling, but there were no answers there. She'd been the architect of her own misfortune, and now it was time to wake up and sort herself out. When it came to men, she was certifiably hopeless. *Learn from that and move on.* Thank goodness she had a career. She wouldn't be making the same mistake twice.

Twice? Make that ever again.

Kimmie had returned to London as fast as she could—which was to say she'd used the ticket she would have used if she'd stayed on for a few days' honeymoon. There was no point wasting money when the trip had already cost so much.

Five months on and she'd heard absolutely nothing from Kris. *That must have been some business trip!* But she wasn't going to dwell on it. She hadn't expected to ever hear from him again.

London always lifted her spirits. She'd given notice on her tiny flat and made appointments to view some more properties. *A new broom sweeps clean,* she determined as she strode through the park on a glorious wintry afternoon.

It was one of those days when London was at its beautiful best beneath a flawless blue sky. The city she loved was crowded and vibrant, with countless different languages floating on the breeze. To Kimmie everything was endlessly fascinating and reassuringly the same.

She was heading for the bank to check out the balance on both her business and personal accounts, to make sure she had enough to put a deposit on a new place and see her through while she continued to build up enough paintings for the exhibition. Mike had signed over his right to manage her finances without a hitch, so there should be enough funds to rent a larger, even cosier home, maybe with a bit of a garden for the baby.

She was feeling optimistic, which was a happy bonus of the show she was planning. Full of laughter and light, it reflected all the good things she'd brought home from Kaimos…including the beloved bump.

Kris.

Her heart yearned for him. She would never forget him. Why hadn't they done a simple thing like exchange phone numbers? She had no idea where he lived in London, or if he stayed in hotels. His private email was just that: private. She'd rung the top hotels, but had drawn a blank. Determined not to be beaten, she ended up using old-fashioned pen and paper, writing and delivering a note to one of the receptionists at his fabulous London offices.

The woman had stared at her sternly, before putting the letter in an in-tray bulging to the brim. Would it get lost? Would the woman remove it once Kimmie had left the building? There were no guarantees. She'd even hung around a while in the hope of seeing Kris until the security guard had politely asked her to leave.

Ships that pass in the night, she mused sadly as she reached the door of the bank. Surely she'd meant more to him than that? Maybe not, and there was nothing to be done about it now. She'd tried to call him too, but had been stonewalled at all his numerous offices. She could imagine Kristof Kaimos received plenty of calls and visits from women and they were all blocked, though not from women carrying his child, she hoped.

She had to forget Kris and get on with her life. She'd known it was never going to be for ever. No promises had been made on either side and it had been obvious he didn't want to be part of her life. If he had, he would have found her by now. Billionaires must have security teams and investigators, but clearly no one had tried to find her.

New life, new start, new everything, Kimmie pledged as she passed through the bank's revolving doors on a wave of determination.

Unfortunately, it didn't prove to be quite that easy.

'I'm sorry. I can't help you with a short-term loan,' the bank manager said flatly.

'But it's only until my next exhibition,' Kimmie explained, feeling numb and faint. 'I need more funds for canvases and paints, and to hire a hall. And I need a deposit for a new place. My paintings are stacked up in every spare inch of space where I'm living at the moment, and I can't carry on like that when my baby's born.' She cradled her bump, already knowing from the look on the manager's face that there would be no new place, and no way of earning the money to pay for one.

'There's no certainty in your profession,' the manager explained, as if Kimmie didn't know this. 'The bank has changed its policy where the arts are concerned.'

Kimmie felt as if her stomach were being turned inside out. 'Surely my past record in selling out an exhibition—'

'Might be a fluke,' the manager interrupted, echoing Kimmie's worst fears. 'I'm really sorry, Ms Lancaster, but there's nothing I can do to help you.'

'Well, thank you for your time,' Kimmie said politely as she forced herself to her feet. 'I'll just transfer some money across from my business account.'

'I'm afraid you can't do that,' the manager said.

'Why not? I can—I must. There has to be some money left,' Kimmie exclaimed, finding it a struggle to remain upbeat.

The manager checked her records. 'It says here that your fiancé signed over all signature rights to you, as per your instruction, but prior to that he emptied the business account. I thought you knew that. At the time of the transaction his was the only signature required, so he had every right to do so.'

The letters from the bank that had remained un-opened while she'd been too busy working to pay much attention to anything outside the drive to paint and paint!

Kimmie had some money in a personal account, which she'd been eking out week to week, but her business account had been under Mike's control since their engagement. That was what they'd agreed. It would take a weight off her shoulders, he'd said. She'd known Mike most of her life and had thought she could trust him.

There was an awkward pause, and then the bank manager stood to indicate that their meeting was over. 'I'm very sorry, Ms Lancaster. I can see this has been a shock for you.'

To put it mildly. But there had to be another op-tion, Kimmie determined, trying to shake off the shock as she left the bank and walked briskly down the street, heading goodness knew where.

There was another option! She'd go to the gallery that held her last exhibition, explain the position she was in and ask if they could possibly help her out in exchange for an increase in the amount of commis-sion they took on each painting.

They might not want to hold the exhibition at all.

True. But it was worth a try.

GALLERY CLOSED

Kimmie stared in disbelief at the sign on the door. Her shoulders slumped. Now she really was beaten.

No money. Nowhere to hold her exhibition. And a baby on the way. She didn't even have enough money for next month's rent on her little flat.

So make a plan.

Based on what? Smoke and mirrors?

Well, standing here fretting wouldn't do any good.

Turning up her collar, she strode off down the street. *When the going gets tough, et cetera, et cetera...*

'No one disappears into thin air,' Kris raged as he paced his London office. 'Someone must know where she is.'

'It's a big city and plenty of people disappear,' his uncle told him with an accepting shrug.

If it hadn't been for Kris's genuine regard for his Uncle Theo, he would have ordered him out of the room. Instead, he was conciliatory. 'Lunch,' he said. 'We'll go out,' he added, when his uncle pulled a face. 'Somewhere nice,' he promised.

Somewhere different...somewhere that might stand a chance of distracting his thoughts from an extraordinary woman with purple-streaked hair, a woman he'd missed more than he could possibly explain...a woman who had cut him off like a dead limb. If Kimmie had wanted to see him, these offices were like a flashing neon sign in the best part of London's business district. She could have left a message or asked to see him. Admittedly, the change-over of receptionists was fast and furious, since any job with Kaimos Shipping was the golden ticket to a better position in a smaller company, but none of them admitted to seeing her. And she was distinctive. How could that have happened?

Quite simply, he concluded with a fierce scowl. Kimmie hadn't wanted to see him, and so she hadn't come near the place.

'You have to find her, Kristof, and sort this out,' his uncle informed him as they boarded the glass lift. 'You're in pain without her, and you're being a pain to everyone you meet. And I include myself in that number,' his uncle snapped as the glass doors slid open to reveal the vast white marble lobby of Kaimos Shipping's London office. 'Start with the college where she studied and work your way forward from there. Think, Kristof. Think like her.'

'Kimmie,' he said. 'Her name is Kimmie Lancaster,' he added tersely as his limo drew up at the kerb. 'And if I thought like Kimmie I'd be the artist in residence here and not the CEO of Kaimos Shipping.'

'Maybe you could learn something from this artistic girl.' His uncle's face softened in sympathy as he climbed into the rear seat. 'She sounds a lot like your aunt, without whom I might have become a bitter tyrant rather than a loving uncle.'

'And a good man,' Kris added with feeling.

'This Kimmie has certainly made an impression on you,' his uncle observed as the sleek black vehicle pulled smoothly into the slow-moving London traffic.

'You could say that,' Kris admitted grimly.

'I've seen a big change in you over the last few months, Kristof.'

He grunted noncommittally.

He was crawling out of his skin with impatience, having drawn a complete blank when it came to Kimmie's whereabouts. Work and calls on his time had piled up remorselessly over the past few months. He'd had to delegate the search, only to end up firing the investigators. He would take charge. A full work diary had always brought him contentment in the past, but Kimmie had changed everything.

Try as he might, nothing could replace her. He'd found himself drifting off in crucial meetings to relive moments with her, and had known then that he'd have no rest until he found her. After the wedding debacle, he could imagine her going to ground to lick her wounds. She wouldn't rely on him. She wouldn't rely on anyone. And she'd be good at hiding. Kimmie had been hiding in one way or another since she was a child. The last thing she'd want would be to inconvenience anyone by unloading her worries on them. What she had to realise was that people who knew her wanted to help her, and he was in pole position where that was concerned.

'Where are we heading now?' his uncle asked querulously as Kris instructed the driver to take a detour on their way to the restaurant. 'I'm hungry and you promised me lunch.'

'And you shall have it, Uncle. As you instructed, I'm trying to think like Kimmie. She didn't leave a number or a forwarding address with Kyria Demetriou, and the investigators seemed sure she didn't have a mortgage, so I'm starting at square one to try and find where she might be renting.'

'Lunch first, then hunt,' his uncle requested. 'I know you're impatient, but an old man needs feeding regularly.'

Grinding his jaw, Kris amended his plan. 'I'll take you to the restaurant, make sure you'll be treated like a king, and I'll leave the car at your disposal.'

His uncle sighed heavily but knew there was no arguing with Kris in this mood. 'Very well,' he agreed grudgingly. 'Do what you must.'

Kris was too fiercely absorbed in his most recent plan to notice the small smile that had crept on to his uncle's face.

The word MEN, with a thick black diagonal warning sign painted through the three bold letters. How good did that feel?

Maybe she'd take up graffiti art, Kimmie mused as she stood back with the brush she'd been using to express her feelings on the canvas poised in one hand. Or not! Black paint was running down the hand in question, and did this really fit with her sun-drenched exhibition—the one that was supposed to make people feel happy?

Taking the canvas off the easel, she stacked it with the rest of the rejects in the one remaining corner of her tiny room. She huffed as she stared at the rejected painting, knowing it was a reaction to her latest knockback by a trendy gallery.

'Sunny?' the snooty owner had exclaimed as if Kimmie had suggested something vile. 'How utterly un-cool,' he'd added with a sneer.

'Not really,' Kimmie had pointed out with a thoughtful expression. 'It's full of sex and heat and naked bodies, so I think you'd call it quite hot.'

'Come back here, young lady. I might be interested—'

'Too late,' she'd called out gaily. She needed someone who was one hundred per cent on board to stand a chance of her exhibition being successful. A lot depended on the buzz being circulated, and as the artist she could only do so much of that.

Undaunted by this latest setback, she quartered the streets of London that she was familiar with, searching for somewhere she could paint, store her work and potentially exhibit it too. She struck gold when she spotted a large notice in the window of a community centre. *Space available*, it read. *Suitable for dance classes, lecture hall or exhibition space.*

Perfect, Kimmie thought as she walked in. Finding the caretaker, a no-nonsense woman called Mandy, she introduced herself. 'I'm an artist,' she explained, 'but I'm afraid I don't have much money, so maybe I could help out as well?'

'So you're familiar with paint?' Mandy asked, wrinkling her nose as if an idea had just come to her.

'Absolutely.'

'This hall needs painting.'

'Ah…' Kimmie smiled. Here was someone who could not only get her out of a mess, but who could give Kimmie a sense of purpose while she did so. 'I'm quite happy to barter my services as decorator in exchange for a reduced cost on the space,' she confirmed.

'Reduced cost?' Mandy exclaimed. 'You can have it for free if you paint the hall. Are you sure you'll have enough time?'

'I'll make time,' Kimmie said, firming her jaw.

'Right then. We've got a deal,' Mandy confirmed. 'I'll close the hall while you're working, and even provide the tea.'

She'd have to make several trips with her paintings, Kimmie reflected, but once the hall was decorated she could hang them in a weekend. This was perfect.

'Thank you so much.'

'Wow…' Mandy breathed on the first day of that weekend. Kimmie had just hung her painting of Kris. Naked on the bed, he was fortunately lying on his stomach. Even so, the sight of him, impossibly masculine, hard-muscled and deeply tanned, indolently displayed to best advantage, was a breath-stealing sight.

'Obviously post-sex, with those bed sheets rumpled around him,' Mandy commented thoughtfully in her usual blunt manner. 'Lucky you,' she added with a twinkle in her eyes as she stared at Kimmie.

'Oh, no. I...'

'Don't even,' Mandy warned, holding up her hand to silence Kimmie, 'because I won't believe you.'

'He's just another man,' Kimmie protested. 'Another subject to paint.'

'Hun,' Mandy said wearily, 'that is *not* "just another man".'

She sighed dramatically. 'That is *the* man, the pinnacle of the expectation of our collective wombs, and it's your duty to share him with the world. I expect he'll sell out first. Who wouldn't want that hanging on their wall?' Standing back to admire the nude of Kris once more, she sighed again. 'And you're good,' she added, turning from the painting to stare at Kimmie. 'You're really good and I believe in you. Don't you think it's time to start believing in yourself?'

CHAPTER ELEVEN

THE PAINTINGS DID look fabulous, thanks to Mandy's help with hanging them. Now all that remained was to spread the word and hope someone turned up. Whatever happened, at least the community hall had had a facelift. Who needed a fancy gallery when Kimmie had a fairy godmother in the comforting shape of Mandy? A second fairy godmother, Kimmie thought wistfully as she remembered Kyria Demetriou and hoped she'd see her again. The bright scenes of Kaimos were largely due to her encouragement. They made Kimmie smile. She could only hope they made everyone else smile too.

'Go home, Kimmie,' Mandy prompted. 'There's nothing more you can do here tonight, and you can leave it to me to lock up.'

'Thanks. The hall looks fabulous, thanks to you.'

'And to your hard work and the exhibition,' Mandy put in, 'and in your condition you need a rest now.'

'I'm pregnant, not sick,' Kimmie protested smiling.

'Even so, I'm taking charge and you're going home,'

Mandy insisted, shooing Kimmie towards the door. 'You want to be fresh for the opening, don't you?'

'If anyone comes,' Kimmie said wryly, hoping they would. She needed to pay the rent this month and, however carefully she budgeted, her small reserve of money had almost run out.

Would anyone come to the wrong side of town?

Fortunately, she'd put a small sum aside to pay for some flyers, which she had posted all over town, including the West End and Knightsbridge, as well as other fashionable areas like the King's Road, Marylebone High Street and Notting Hill. Literally anyone who had agreed to take one of her carefully designed posters showing just a snapshot of her work had been thanked from the bottom of her heart before she'd moved on.

The miles of walking had done her good. As she'd criss-crossed the wintry streets of London, she had realised how kind people could be. Some had even expressed an interest in coming along to the exhibition, so perhaps it wouldn't be a washout after all.

Meeting Mandy had been the key to everything, Kimmie mused as she hugged her friend and said goodnight. On her way out, she gazed up at her painting of Kris and smiled. She couldn't help herself. Perhaps his uncle wouldn't want Kris naked on his wall, but there were the earlier sketches as well as the finished painting of Kris, looking hard and driven and every bit the commanding CEO. Perhaps they could hang that one on the boardroom wall in one of his offices.

'Now, don't you worry about anything,' Mandy insisted as she opened the door and an icy draught blew in. 'I'll make sandwiches and tea for everyone tomorrow.' And when Kimmie protested that they didn't even know if anyone would come, she added, 'Spending a lot of money on paintings will be hungry work, I expect, so I'd better stock up and get cracking first thing in the morning.'

Nothing she could say would put her friend off. Maybe it was time she took the same line, Kimmie thought as Mandy added, 'Those beautiful posters are enough to charm the birds from the trees. We'll be turning people away. Your work is fabulous. I predict you'll be a sell-out. I'll make sure there's water, as well as decaf tea for you, so you've no excuse not to enjoy the event to the full, and make a lot of money.'

'I can't thank you enough,' Kimmie said as they parted at the door.

'Think about what you've done for us…for the community,' Mandy called after her. 'It was a lucky day for everyone when you knocked on the door, and we'll all be here to support you.'

Yes, Kimmie thought as she strode out. This wouldn't be a terrifying snooty event like her first exhibition, but an event full of warmth and love, where wonderful, genuine people would surround her. She didn't have to dress up in stiff, awkward clothes and try to be someone else. She could be Kimmie and relax.

* * *

London was vast and, even with the meagre clues he had to follow, it wasn't easy to find a definite lead. But when he had almost given up for the day, and was heading home to his town house behind Harrods, he saw a flyer in a small art shop window.

He'd found her!

The shock of it had been like a punch to his solar plexus. He'd been flying ever since. But he wouldn't rush this. He had to get it right or she'd no doubt find some way to disappear again. Stubborn, proud and independent, Kimmie belonged to no one, and was all the more desirable for that.

The thought that after all this time he would be seeing her tomorrow had made for a sleepless night, and the next day had been spent pacing his office, refusing all calls. Eventually, he deemed it time to go home, shower and change into something more relaxed…more Kimmie, more appropriate for a sunny, upbeat exhibition in a community hall.

Her choice of venue made him smile. It was so Kimmie, he reflected as he parked the shave in favour of leaving a few minutes earlier than he'd planned. She'd probably been turned down by all the regular galleries, and had marched on undaunted. She could always be relied upon to do the unexpected. Wasn't that the essence of her charm?

Unbelievable. The line of people waiting patiently for Kimmie's exhibition to open stretched down the road as far as she could see through the front window of the community hall, and there were quite a few faces she recognised from her first exhibition. What meant even more was the fact that it wasn't just a gathering of photographers and celebrities and assorted glitterati jostling on the pavement waiting for the doors to open, but what seemed to Kimmie to be the entire neighbourhood turning out to support her.

'This is amazing,' she exclaimed, turning to Mandy. 'I just can't believe it—I can't tell you how much it means to me. How did you get people to come?'

'You got them to come,' Mandy said as they peered through the window together. 'They're here for you, Kimmie, and for your art. You've done so much for us, working late into the night to redecorate and brighten up this centre, and nothing goes unnoticed here.'

When they opened the doors the big hall was full to capacity right away. What amazed Kimmie even more was the fact that the sticky red dots Mandy was putting on frames to show that a picture was sold quickly covered most of the exhibition. Soon there wouldn't be anything left to buy…except for the huge canvases of Kris, which as yet hadn't sold.

No! They had sold too, she noticed on her next inspection. Both the portrait of Kris in profile and the initial sketch she'd made, as well as the huge nude of him, had red dots in the corner of each frame.

Insanely, she now felt a pang of jealousy. Who was going to hang naked Kris on their wall? She didn't want to part with him and would just have to explain to the prospective purchaser that there'd been a mistake and that certain canvases weren't for sale.

Who'd agreed the price, anyway? she wondered as she frowned and stroked her bump. These were the only two paintings without prices attached, and they were both of Kris. She couldn't explain why that had happened... Well, she could—she had never really wanted to sell the images of Kris in the first place.

Turning, she searched the room for Mandy, hoping her fairy godmother would be able to tell her who had put in the offer to buy them, and how much they'd paid. She'd have to refund it, of course, but it couldn't be helped. Plenty of other paintings had sold, more than enough to see her through financially, if she was really careful, for the whole of next year.

Nothing could have prepared him for seeing Kimmie again. The shock of realising she was pregnant took even longer to process. *His baby?* Of course it was his baby. Furious with himself for even harbouring doubt for a moment, he drank her in like a man finding water in the desert. Even beneath her shapeless dungarees, which she wore with one strap hanging down and the top half askew and paint-streaked, it was obvious she was quite a few months pregnant. Pregnant and proud.

The scale of the hall made her appear smaller and more fragile than he remembered, but that was deceptive. Physically, Kimmie might be vulnerable, but her spirit was pure tempered steel. From her tousled purple-streaked hair cascading way past her waist to the tip of her trainers-clad feet she was everything he remembered, and now so much more.

She was staring up at his portrait and appeared deep in thought. It was a kick in the teeth to see himself through Kimmie's eyes in that first sketch she'd ever made of him, now a life-size painting. He appeared so harsh and unforgiving, with his jaw set and his eyes fierce, his mouth firmed in an intolerant line. There was no humour or tenderness to be seen. Was that what she actually thought of him?

A great well of feeling opened up inside him as she stroked her bump. The unconscious gesture touched him somewhere deep, somewhere he didn't even know he had. Was she introducing their child to its father, or making a vow to keep them apart?

He hadn't realised how much he'd missed her, or how much seeing her again would affect him. Both elated and stunned now he knew she was pregnant, he wasn't sure of the reception he'd receive. Kimmie had gone to ground for reasons he believed had nothing to do with him or the pregnancy. His best guess was she just wanted to get on with her life. And why shouldn't she? Why should she think any more of him than her ex-fiancé? He'd given her no reason to feel reassured. Business had always come first for him, and he'd been away from her for so much longer than he'd ever intended, though once he was back in London he'd launched a futile search for her right away.

Angry with himself for even wasting a moment,

it was as if every emotion he'd suppressed for years came flooding back all at once. Discovering they were going to have a child together had rocked his foundations. The thought of becoming a father filled him with fire and love, and an overwhelming need to provide and protect. He had to do better than his parents. He must. He would.

'Kimmie…'

She turned slowly as if she needed a moment to accept that she really was hearing his voice.

'Kris?' she whispered, staring up at him in disbelief. 'What are you doing here?'

'Fulfilling my promise to you,' he said with a shrug, when what he felt like doing was dragging her into his arms and kissing her hard with sheer relief, and what he felt like saying was, *Did you imagine I could stay away?*

She took him in, from the top of his wild, uncombed hair, to the abundance of stubble on his face, and on to his black winter boots, heavy jacket and jeans. Once he'd discovered Kimmie's whereabouts, he'd barely drawn a level breath. It had been hard enough waiting until her exhibition opened without wasting time on thinking how he looked. Like a vagabond, he guessed, remembering how she'd loved to rub herself against his stubble.

A faint pink flush came to her cheeks as she admitted, 'I didn't think you'd bother.'

'I've been searching for you. You've become quite elusive.'

She didn't deny it and, after a few tense seconds, she caressed her stomach and said, 'As you can see, we need to talk.'

'Yes, we do,' he agreed.

'I'm afraid I can't spare the time yet...' She glanced around. 'Has anyone offered you a cup of tea?'

'No, but I'm fine without one. I'll wait for you.'

'Have something to eat,' she pressed, leading the way to a buffet table laden with delicious-looking home-made fare. He guessed this had been donated by Kimmie's loyal supporters, judging by the warm greetings and glances coming her way.

'Have you just flown in? You must be tired,' she said.

'I have a house in London.'

'Oh...yes...yes, of course. So you found me,' she added, clearly uncertain as to his feelings for her.

'Appears so,' he agreed, noting how she nursed her belly as she stared at him. 'Happy news,' he said firmly, wanting to put his stake in the ground. 'I wish I'd known sooner, but that business issue was more problematic than I'd thought.'

'So you didn't get my note,' she said.

He frowned. 'What note?'

'The note I left with your receptionist in London when I couldn't get hold of you any other way.'

'I haven't received a note.'

He couldn't bear that they were talking in such an abbreviated form, like two strangers discussing the weather.

'I want you to know how thrilled I am.' Even that

seemed inadequate, when what he wanted to do was to throw back his head and roar with happiness, and with confidence in the future. His natural impatience overcame his plan to play it cool. 'How soon can you leave?' he asked.

'The exhibition?' Kimmie frowned. 'I can't.'

'You're not going to stay here all night, are you?'

'No,' she agreed, 'but I don't want to keep you hanging around, and I can't say what time we'll be locking up. We can't leave until the last guest has left the building.'

'We?' A bolt of suspicion hit him like a freight train. It had never occurred to him that there might be someone else in the picture.

'Mandy, the caretaker, and me,' Kimmie explained, smiling faintly as if she'd guessed the track his thoughts were taking. 'I won't leave Mandy to clear up on her own, and I don't want to rush anyone out of here. To be honest, I really shouldn't be talking to you now.'

'When, then?' he bit out, finally noticing that a queue of people, all wanting to speak to the artist, had formed behind him. Timing was everything in business; Kimmie had created an uplifting exhibition in challenging times and she was obviously very much in demand. To maximise sales and guarantee future commissions, she had to strike while the iron was hot. 'Text me when you're done,' he demanded as she stared at him and raised a brow.

'I don't have your number,' she reminded him coolly.

'You don't…?' Cursing his own stupidity silently, he pulled out his phone. 'Here—take it now.'

Maybe his tone was a little terse, but she made no attempt to do as he asked. Instead she said, 'Are you sure you wouldn't like to put a tag in my ear too?'

'I beg your pardon?'

'Kris, you can't speak to me like that. You can't walk back into my life after months apart as if nothing's happened and claim me like just another of your properties. Your business trip is finally over and you're at a loose end. I get that. But I came home determined to pick up my career, and that's what I've done. At the moment things are going really well but, with a baby on the way, I have to maintain the momentum. I can't drop everything just because it suits you.'

'If not today, then tomorrow,' he said, hardly believing he was prepared to wait, but he could hardly tear her away from such a successful event. Nor could he hang around like a spare part. 'I'll send my driver to pick you up.'

'You're too busy?' she suggested bluntly.

'No. It's just…'

'The way things are done in your world?' she supplied when he fell short of an answer.

It *was* the way things were done in his world. So his world would have to change.

'Give me a time, and I'll pick you up myself.'

'Don't bother; I'm quite capable of meeting you anywhere you choose.'

'I want to pick you up. Is that clear enough, you infuriating woman?' he ground out.

'You're sure business won't call you away again?'

The way she asked did more than hint at hurt and loss of trust, and it was a warning not to mess this up.

'My business is here with you,' he stated firmly.

She gave him a long, considering stare, while he wanted nothing more than to give her that loving hug she'd asked for all those months ago. Following his instinct and drawing her into his arms, he held her close. Inhaling deeply, he absorbed her light floral scent. In her artist's dungarees splashed with paint, Kimmie looked every inch the creative genius, but underneath that façade he knew she was vulnerable and alone. She needed him as much as he needed her, and not just because she was expecting his child—a child who would eventually inherit the Kaimos Shipping line—but because they were better together than apart. Without her, he was nothing. Life was bland and colourless. He hadn't realised just how much she meant to him until now.

Before he knew it, she'd pulled away.

'Kimmie…'

Too late. She was already swallowed up in the crowd. Fuming at missed opportunities, he wasn't in the best of moods when the caretaker, Mandy, appeared at his side.

'Kimmie says she'd like to meet you here tomorrow, and then go to a nearby café to talk.'

'She couldn't tell me that herself?'

'Mr Kaimos. This is Kimmie's moment. Please

don't deny her what she's worked so hard for. She's done so much good here in such a short time— offering free art classes, painting the hall. We owe her, and I can't stand by and let anyone take that away. Don't be too proud to accept her suggestion. Meet her at eleven tomorrow morning, when she's had the chance to absorb what's happened here today.'

'Eleven tomorrow,' he called out as Mandy walked away. But this was the last time he'd go through an intermediary, and Kimmie needed to know that.

Hearing the tension in his voice, Mandy turned. 'You're both wounded. Give yourselves the chance to heal.'

This wasn't over yet. It had only just begun.

CHAPTER TWELVE

No. No. No. She couldn't do this again. The way she had felt when she'd seen Kris again was too extreme, too big, too life-changing. It was as if everything had come into sharp focus, making the world a bigger, brighter place. Unfortunately, she already knew that such things were fantasies that could all come crashing down, and did she want to risk that again? Could she, with a baby to consider?

Having taken refuge in Mandy's office, and having passed the buck to Mandy when it came to telling Kris that she would agree to meet him here at the community centre tomorrow morning at eleven, she was not only feeling pathetic for hiding away but wondering if she'd made the biggest mistake yet in agreeing to see him again. What was he going to do? Pat her on the back and write a cheque? She didn't want his financial help in raising their child. She didn't want his financial help full stop. What she should do now was go and find him and tell him they could meet at a lawyer's office to discuss the details. She could just text him and cancel. She had his number…

Kimmie went as far as pulling out her phone before realising how ridiculous she was being. Having a child with Kris wasn't something she wanted to run away from, even if she could. They were two rational human beings and they could have a civilised discussion like anyone else.

Sitting back in Mandy's chair, she stuffed the phone back into her pocket and closed her eyes. That almost made things worse, because now she could feel her heart aching because she'd seen him again, while her body was behaving disgracefully. It was a need only Kris could fill and though to have him back was like a light switching on, when he left he'd take another piece of her heart, and what about their baby? How would she explain that sort of behaviour to their child? *Oh, your father will see you again when he's got time*? There was nothing more important in all the world than this baby, and she would protect their child with her life, even from Kris if she had to.

Deny their child the other half of its heritage? Could she really do that?

She must stand up to Kris to stop him taking over. And she could do it, because it was time, as Mandy had said, for Kimmie to believe in herself.

Returning to the hall, she tried to find him in the throng, but it was hopeless trying to see over people's heads. Increasingly frustrated, she had to act normally for the sake of everyone who was here to support her, but it was hard to concentrate with pic-

tures of Kris hanging on the walls. All she'd wanted
was to throw herself into his arms and welcome him
back so they could share the happiness of expecting a child together, but doubt remained as to how
long he'd stay and while that stood between them
she couldn't—wouldn't—expose herself and their
child to future hurt.

'He's gone.'

'I'm sorry?' Kimmie stared blankly at Mandy.

'He paid for the paintings and left.'

'Which paintings?' Kimmie shook her head in
bewilderment.

'He bought the nude of himself on that rumpled bed as well as the portrait. And he paid a lot of
money for them,' Mandy added with obvious delight.
'I explained that I wasn't sure of the price, but when
he mentioned a figure I knew you wouldn't want me
to refuse. The portrait's for his uncle, he said, while
the nude was for private consumption only. Don't
worry,' she added as Kimmie frowned. 'He smiled
as he said that, so I think he took it well.'

'And now he's gone?' she said, not wanting to believe it as she looked around again.

'Yes,' Mandy confirmed. 'And we'd better start
circulating again. There are people waiting to speak
to you, and others wanting to pay. I'm guessing this
is going to be your second sell-out show.'

Mandy's happy words of triumph echoed somewhere in Kimmie's head, but all she was aware of,
really, was that Kris had gone again. Why had he

left? What did it signify? Was he pleased about the baby? Indifferent? Or was he already making plans to consult his lawyers?

He's doing as you asked, stupid. He's agreed to meet you tomorrow, and he's confirmed with Mandy that he will.

Kris Kaimos doing as Kimmie Lancaster said? Did that seem likely? Or was he giving her a chance to realise that she couldn't fight him?

Stop! You'll find out the answer at eleven o'clock tomorrow morning.

If he turned up.

Of course he'll turn up. Can you imagine Kristof Kaimos shying away from anything?

Well, he'd better, or she'd text him until her phone exploded. They must talk before he left town again, and make plans for the future of their child.

Could they do that over hot chocolate in a bustling London café?

Yes. They'd have to. Communication was key. Everything hinged on how Kris felt about becoming a parent. She could manage without him, and might have to; there were no guarantees. He might not want to have a child, and she did. For as long as she could remember, Kimmie had learned not to want, to wish, to hope, but becoming pregnant had changed everything. She wanted the world for her baby, and wanted all her child's wishes to come true. If she could just steer their baby onto the path of happiness she'd be content, because that was the most important goal of all.

Kris called to her in other ways, Kimmie mused as she moved about the hall, chatting to one group and then the next. He had claimed her heart in a way she couldn't explain, but with a baby to raise, a life to lead and a career to nurture if she was to support them both, she had to look out for herself and must never rely on the temptation that was Kristof Kaimos. Business would always come first for him. If they became close again, how long would it be before he left on another business trip? And would she become as commonplace and as interchangeable as a piece of his real estate? For the sake of their child, she couldn't allow that to happen. Talking in a busy café was a great idea. They could have a drink and a chat, and sketch out some plans—if he wanted to be involved. Or would a regular bank transfer be more to his liking, if not to hers?

Of course he wanted to be involved! His eyes had lit up when he'd seen her and realised she was pregnant. No one could fake that type of response. Kris might be hard and driven in business but, just as Kimmie hid her true self beneath countless protective onion skins of reckless boho attitude, she was still learning the lessons of the past. Kris was the same; he had many more layers than he showed to the world. Kimmie understood him because their pasts were so similar in a way, but that didn't mean she had to roll over at his every demand. Anyway, it was no use fretting about it. Her questions would be answered tomorrow.

* * *

She was even more beautiful than he remembered. And punctual. He was early. He couldn't wait to see her again, and would have chosen his Harley to whip through the sluggish London traffic, but Kimmie was quite advanced in her pregnancy so he had chosen the slower option of an SUV. 'Ready?' he asked, impatient to the last.

'I thought we were going there to talk,' she said, pointing down the road to where a neon sign was flashing above a nearby café.

'We can if you'd rather?' He shrugged.

'No,' she said, glancing at the sleek black SUV. 'If you promise to keep me and the bump safe I'm happy to let you drive us somewhere further away.'

'Us,' he said as he helped her in.

'Us,' she confirmed as he joined her.

Kris smiled as he gunned the engine. He had a good feeling about this, and it grew as he sensed rather than saw Kimmie rest back against the seat. She had no clue where they were going, but nothing fazed her and he was confident that the same would apply to the question he had to ask.

'This is amazing,' she exclaimed as they swept across Waterloo Bridge.

'Not too fast for you?' he asked as he brought the vehicle to a halt alongside a simple pop-up food outlet located on the bank of the Thames.

'Perfect,' she said, seeming delighted as she gazed around. 'I love London, even in winter. These flawless blue skies remind me of Greece.'

'It's a bit colder here,' he commented.

'So long as the sun's shining, I don't care,' she said. 'Hmm. That food smells good, and I'm starving. Eating for two,' she reminded him.

'Hot dog? Hamburger?'

'Don't you just love the contrast of colourful food shack and Old Father Thames drifting to the sea like a dirty old rag?'

'Stop thinking about painting and tell me what you want to eat,' he prompted. When Kimmie was in this mood it was hard to be impatient with her.

With a smile, she looked at him. 'I love surprise adventures. This has been fun,' she admitted, a wistful note creeping into her voice.

'And it isn't over yet,' he reminded her, unable to keep a stern note out of his tone. They had to discuss the baby. Yesterday had been fraught. She'd been too shocked to see him to say much, and the event had taken up all her time, but once they'd had something to eat he was going to drill down into the detail of what would happen next.

'I think we should get married,' he said bluntly after two steaming hot drinks and a belly full of food.

'I'm sorry?' Kimmie looked startled. 'Seriously?' She frowned when he produced a velvet box from the inner pocket of his jacket.

'Of course I'm being serious,' he said, obviously affronted. This was not the reaction he'd expected.

'Aren't you jumping the gun?' she commented with a huff of surprise. 'We haven't even talked about the future yet.'

'Do we need to?'

'Of course we do,' she insisted with an incredulous look.

'How much discussion does this need?' Flipping the catch, he revealed a priceless blue diamond circled by brilliant cut pure blue-whites, each the carat weight of most people's conservatively sized engagement ring jewel.

'Quite a lot, I'd say,' she told him sharply.

'Have you even looked at this magnificent jewel?'

'I don't need to look at it,' she said through gritted teeth.

'Well, if I didn't get it right I'll buy you something else.'

'I don't want anything at all. I'm not ready—maybe I never will be,' she added, wringing her hands. 'Look, do you want the truth,' she demanded, 'or shall I sugarcoat it?'

'Just give me your answer,' he said impatiently. 'I can't believe there's a problem.'

'Believe it,' she said fiercely. 'This is all wrong. It's as wrong as it could be. You're only doing this because of the baby.'

'No, I'm not,' he protested. 'I want you to be my wife.'

'To spend the rest of my life with you? To grow old together?'

Truthfully, he hadn't thought that far ahead.

'When you can spare the time, that is,' she added with an ironic look.

The sad look in her eyes held him to account.

'You're not being fair,' he protested. 'What you say isn't true. I've got all the time in the world for you.'

'So your business will suddenly run itself?'

He ground his jaw. 'I'll learn to delegate,' he offered finally.

'Really?' she commented with a disbelieving look.

'Why not?'

'I'll take more convincing than a ride in your SUV and a hot dog on the bank of the Thames.'

'I'll buy you anything you want,' he offered. 'Just name it.'

'You just don't get it, do you?' she said. The sad look had returned to her face. 'I don't want anything from you. I don't want hasty solutions either. I can look after myself.'

'But you don't have to.'

'Don't I?' Her look this time was steady and penetrating.

'It won't be what you think,' he assured her. 'I know you. I know what you need—'

'You think you do,' she cut in, 'but if you really knew me you wouldn't have bought me a ring like that.'

'I want to show you what's possible.'

'A piece of jewellery like that doesn't show me anything, apart from the fact that you have a lot of money.'

He shrugged. 'Then choose another one.'

'Will that keep me warm at night? Will it make me feel safe and cherished and loved?'

'It should do,' he insisted.

'So that's your reassurance?' she said sadly. 'If I accept this ring I'll be happy, because lots of money buys lots of happiness and security for me and our child. Is that your best argument?'

'Yes. Why not? What are you doing?' he demanded tensely as she moved to the edge of the kerb.

'Hailing a cab,' she informed him as she held out her hand.

'There's absolutely no need for you to do that when I'll take you back.'

Turning to face him, she said steadily, 'There's every need to do this. Get in touch again when you've had a chance to think things through. We really do need to talk. And, Kris…?' She glanced at the black velvet box he was still holding, containing the ring he'd had specially made for Kimmie, paying the royal jeweller to stay up all night to finish work on the setting. 'Valuable rings aren't the answer. Don't you remember I discovered that in Kaimos?'

She was comparing him to her ex, and that bit of tin he'd given her to Kris's extravagant display of commitment? Now he was mad. But Kimmie didn't give him the chance to express his feelings. A black cab had swept to her side at the kerb. The driver lowered the window and she told him where she wanted to go. The next moment she was slamming the door. Just before it closed, she called out, 'I'll wait to hear from you. And thanks for breakfast.'

And then she was gone.

Was this some sort of test? She'd wait to hear from

him? What was that supposed to mean? He was supposed to chase her? He was halfway home before he'd even begun to calm down. To say there was a lot of thinking to do would be a massive understatement.

Kimmie felt numb on the drive back home, and her hand shook as she put the key in the lock of her flat. What a mess. Two individuals, worlds apart, struggling to find some common ground so they could talk about the child they were expecting. How could they ever work things out? They had to. A child was too big a topic, too big a love to shove to one side and leave to another day. They both knew how it felt to long for love and be denied the smallest recognition. But she wasn't going to waste a second on looking back. Shedding her jacket, she plopped down on the bed-settee and pulled out her phone. They had to arrange to talk. They must make arrangements to meet again, and soon.

Kimmie smiled ruefully. Before she'd even had the chance to call Kris, his name flashed up on her screen.

'Dinner tonight,' he suggested when she answered. 'We need to talk.'

'Just what I was thinking,' she admitted. 'I was on the point of calling you.'

'I'll send a car.'

This time she didn't argue. 'What time?'

'Eight.'

'Perfect.'

His tone was neutral. Hers was too.

* * *

From Kimmie's limited wardrobe, she chose a simple long-sleeved deep blue midi-dress, which she teamed with black ankle boots. Not a sequin in sight. No bells. No tassels. Smart, but still a little quirky. She couldn't change her style for Kris. Where would he take her for dinner? Neutral territory, she hoped, somewhere quiet and discreet where they could have a proper talk.

A uniformed chauffeur arrived promptly at eight o'clock. She appreciated Kris's businesslike approach to a pressing problem. No pressure, no panic, just a calm and considered solution. The limousine was sleek, black and super-luxurious, and the driver negotiated the London traffic almost as smoothly as Kris had. Other people on the roads tended to make way for such an impressive-looking vehicle, she soon discovered. Staring out of the window as they halted at traffic lights, she saw one of her flyers still displayed in a shop window, and realised that was how Kris had found her. Moving off again, they drove for a few more miles until eventually the limo drew to a halt outside one of London's finest hotels.

A doorman approached and helped her out. Entering the brilliantly-lit lobby with its muted sound palette and incredible floral displays, she was glad Kris had chosen neutral territory. Yet she was still wary because this was his neutral territory, a place where he felt at home and where she felt hopelessly unstylish in her cheap maternity clothes.

'This way, madam,' a smartly dressed woman invited. 'Your friend is waiting for you in the private dining room.'

Naturally, Kris would be there already, no doubt champing at the bit. The most important thing was to keep her wits about her tonight. She must not allow her feelings for him to overrule her common sense.

As soon as she entered the private room, Kris stood. The table was beautifully decorated with flowers and crystal and silver cutlery. Two waiters hovered in the background, while champagne was chilling in an ice bucket, alongside a bottle of sparkling water for Kimmie. He'd thought of everything. Did that make him ruthless and determined, or caring and concerned? There was only one way to find out.

The waiter held her chair and she sat down opposite Kris, who looked amazing. Of course he did. When did Kris look anything but amazing? Tonight he was wearing an exquisitely tailored dark suit that pointed up his incredible physique. He'd teamed this with a crisp white shirt and a discreetly coloured pale grey silk tie. He was the embodiment of style and sophistication. Or appeared to be. Only she knew about the tattoos beneath that sharp suit, and the glint of an earring almost concealed by his thick, wavy black hair. Beneath his apparent sophistication, Kris was as unconventional as Kimmie. It could be said that neither of them truly belonged in this most traditional of settings, but Kris had made it his own, and so would she.

'Thank you for coming to see me,' he said politely.

'I'm pleased to be here,' she said with matching reserve.

The ritual of eating went without a hitch. The food was delicious and conversation, though stilted at first, eventually flowed easily.

'I'm not who you think I am,' Kris said calmly as they waited for hot drinks to arrive, coffee for him and fresh mint tea for Kimmie. 'The ring was a mistake, I see that now.'

Kimmie shrugged as she admitted, 'But it was a very kind thought. And as for who I think you are...? Honestly? My opinion changes by the minute. I'm still getting to know you,' she explained.

'Which was why the ring was too much too soon?' Kris asked, watching her carefully.

'That ring would always be too much for me. Imagine it covered in paint,' she exclaimed. 'And it was definitely offered at a point in my life where I just don't know you well enough to commit to a life-long arrangement.'

'An arrangement?' he echoed sharply.

'For the sake of our child.'

'I stand admonished,' he said with a sudden smile that lit up his eyes.

She wanted to believe him, but did Kris do anything without a good reason? Why did he need to make her his wife? They could still be good parents to their child without making that final commitment to each other, couldn't they?

'I've kept the ring,' he advised, 'so if you change your mind...'

'I won't,' she assured him.

'Then keep it as a dress ring. I'll give it to you, no strings attached.'

'Thank you.' She shook her head firmly. 'But no. Better you return it and get your money back. Or keep it for the next contender.'

'I sincerely hope you're joking,' he said with a scowl.

Deep down, so did she.

'All I'm asking is that you consider marriage for the sake of our child,' he pressed.

'A piece of paper won't make any difference. All our child needs is our love.'

'Ah, if only life were that simple.' Kris sighed.

'You make it sound like just another business deal,' Kimmie observed, feeling her heart twist in anguish. Was it wrong to want so much more?

'Marriage is a business deal of sorts,' Kris argued.

Was he right? Kimmie was beginning to doubt her own judgement. The only way she could unscramble her brain was by concentrating on their baby. Then again, if this was the first time either of them had discussed marriage, they wouldn't have it down pat.

'Let's leave it for now,' Kris suggested, 'and enjoy each other's company for the rest of the evening.'

Could they?

'You'd like that, wouldn't you?'

So much he had no idea.

And Kris made it possible. He wasn't just the consummate businessman, but a consummate charmer too. And so good-looking she could have stared at him for ever as he talked and soothed and seduced.

With a mind like a steel trap, he kept her endlessly entertained and by the end of the evening she was relaxed and happy, and ready to agree to just about anything. Kris was a sexy, highly entertaining man and somehow he'd even managed to halfway convince her that marriage to him would be wonderful. She'd have more freedom, not less. But was that an illusion too? she wondered as he held her chair as they left the table. She was used to making her own money, not relying on anyone else.

Admittedly, she was a bit short at the moment. Some of the profit from the recent exhibition would pay for a new place to rent, but the rest had been safely put away to build her scholarship fund for struggling artists. She couldn't marry Kris and say, *Woo-hoo! I'm in the money now!* It wasn't her way. Standing on her own two feet without anyone propping her up wasn't just a way of life—it was Kimmie's life.

'Everyone needs someone, Kimmie.'

She turned to stare at Kris as they walked out of the room. 'Think about when you have the baby,' he added persuasively. 'You're going to need some help then.'

'Lots of women manage on their own,' she pointed out.

'But you don't have to.'

'And you don't have an ulterior motive in coming up with this sudden proposal of marriage?' she pressed.

'Why would I?' he said with an easy shrug.

But he'd paused before answering. Had her question thrown him? 'I don't know why you'd do it,'

Kimmie admitted. 'Perhaps because you need an heir for your company, and a son for you?'

He gave her a sideways look. 'Or a daughter,' he corrected her.

Having successfully shifted the awkward conversation on to a safer track, he added, 'Now who's being blinkered? I might be many things, but no one could accuse me of being a dinosaur.'

'Of course not,' Kimmie agreed. 'It was just a figure of speech,' she said quietly.

'If you've got time,' he said as they crossed the lobby, 'I'd like you to meet my uncle. Perhaps he can reassure you.'

'As to your motives in proposing to me?'

'As to my good character,' Kris said dryly. 'He's in town at the moment, so it's a great opportunity for the two of you to meet.'

'So he can give his opinion on my suitability as a wife?' she challenged lightly.

'You are suspicious,' Kris countered with a shrug and a sideways look.

Maybe with good reason, Kimmie thought bitterly.

'Anyway, I've made the offer,' Kris told her as they approached the door. 'It's up to you whether or not you accept it.'

She frowned thoughtfully.

'Bed?' he said.

Kimmie blinked as she glanced at the bank of lifts. Was he serious?

'You look tired,' Kris added. 'You should probably go back home now.'

Ah. Okay. She breathed a silent sigh of relief, though her body was less enthusiastic about the way things had turned out. Sensibly, she reasoned the gulf between them was too wide to ever consider staying together permanently and, however charming Kris's uncle might be, nothing could persuade Kimmie to change her mind. It was too soon in every way possible. The wall around her heart was just as high, while her determination to remain independent remained unchanged.

'I'll pick you up tomorrow,' he said, 'and we'll walk through the park if it's sunny. A good dose of fresh air is what we both need to get things out in the open and talk.'

Would Kris get things out in the open?

'I've had a lovely evening,' she said as they walked outside to where his limo was waiting.

'My driver will take you home. I'll stay here tonight,' he explained. 'I have a suite,' he added.

Of course he had a suite. And a town house in London, by all accounts. That gulf between them wasn't just wide, it was unbridgeable, and she was a fool to imagine otherwise, to hope things could be different.

'Tomorrow,' he said as he helped her into the car.

'Tomorrow,' she confirmed, feeling a rush of excitement in spite of her nagging doubt. Kris in charming mode was irresistible, and shouldn't a truly independent woman be free to follow her heart?

CHAPTER THIRTEEN

To hell with that, he thought just as his driver closed his door and buckled up.

'Wait! I'm coming with you.'

Kimmie was speechless, which was just as well. He didn't want to waste time talking. Telling the driver to head for his town house rather than Kimmie's flat, he raised the privacy panel and settled back. They were completely enclosed and private in a vehicle with blacked-out windows. The consequences of that were inevitable. Neither of them needed to speak. Hunger suppressed too long required an outlet. They reached for each other at exactly the same time. No thought went into it as they grappled and tugged at each other's clothes. His hand was where he needed it to be...on Kimmie's plump warmth, while her two hands were wrapped firmly around his erection.

'Not yet... Let me,' she said, sliding onto her knees on the carpeted floor.

This wasn't a request, he gathered, but an instruction. Pressing back against the seat, he opened his legs wide so she could kneel between them. Wrapping her mouth around him, she sucked and licked while he laced his fingers through her hair to keep her close. He had no need to bind her in any way at all, as Kimmie made it plain that she had no intention of going anywhere.

'Pleasuring you gives me pleasure,' she told him as she paused to take a breath. 'How responsive you are. I love that!'

Groaning rhythmically, he hardened still more beneath her increasingly skilful attention. 'You're very good at this,' he observed.

'Are you surprised when I have the very best of subjects to work on?'

She smiled and continued, barely breaking the insistent rhythm until finally he couldn't hold back any longer and thrust deeply and repeatedly into her eager mouth. It took a long time for his breathing to steady, and when it had he helped her onto the seat beside him. 'Your turn now,' he said.

'Oh, that's really not necessary,' she protested.

'But I say it is.'

'Okay,' she agreed on an excited, shaking breath. She gasped as he found her with the slightly roughened pad of his forefinger. He knew exactly what she needed—how fast, how firm—and he wasn't disappointed by her immediate response. 'Again?' he suggested. 'I'll take the edge off your hunger, then rouse you again when we reach the house. There's no need to wait,' he insisted. 'In fact, don't wait,' he added as the limousine turned off the main road and onto a wide, elegant square. 'You'll need to be quick,' he warned.

'And you don't think that's possible?' she asked him in the same shaking voice.

'I do. You can and you will,' he promised, and both delicately and intuitively he made sure that was the case.

She bucked wildly as pleasure surged through her in a series of powerful clenches. He held her firmly in place until she'd finished, and even then little aftershocks continued that made her shake and moan rhythmically. The moans became contented groans just as the limousine drew to a halt.

'Perfect timing,' he said as the engine was switched off. 'Now straighten your clothes,' he instructed briskly, 'and I'll reward you again just as soon as we're in the house.'

'Promise?' she whispered.

'You have my word,' he pledged.

After thanking the driver, Kris opened the front door for Kimmie, closed it behind them and switched on the lights. That was the signal for them to lunge towards each other. 'I want to watch you,' he growled. 'Gently, because of the baby,' he warned when her fingers bit into him.

'Yes,' she gasped as he helped her to scramble up him.

Supporting her with his big hands on her buttocks, Kris buffeted her repeatedly against the door. The sensation was incredible, like nothing she'd ever experienced before.

'Lean on me,' he invited in a husky whisper. 'Don't think about anything but pleasure. Leave everything to me.'

How tempting was that? Irresistible. Like Kris, Kimmie reflected in the nanosecond left to her before she lost control.

Kimmie slept in his arms. She was totally exhausted, he realised as he stroked her tangled hair away from her face. First, the exhibition of her paintings, and then him turning up, as well as carrying a baby, and the passion that bound them together had also taken its toll. She looked so innocent and vulnerable as she lay completely relaxed beside him. Could he find a better wife? But persuading Kimmie he'd make an ideal husband and the best of fathers for their child might be a little harder to pull off. For the first time he could remember, thanks to Kimmie, his personal life was extraordinary, but her independent and unpredictable nature meant he couldn't guarantee the future.

Leaving her to sleep, he went to take a shower. Throwing on jeans and a fine-knit top, he went downstairs to call his uncle so he could arrange to go over to see him with Kimmie. He was confident that Uncle Theo's genial nature would win her over when it came to joining the family.

'I think you're going to like her,' he told his uncle. 'Yes, it's been a bit of a whirlwind,' he conceded, 'but, as you said, it's what I need—and wasn't it the same for you? Plus she's already pregnant,' he added.

He waited for his uncle's reaction, which was more muted than anticipated. 'Are you sure, Kristof?' Theo said at last. 'You know what you mean to me, and I couldn't bear for you to be hurt again.'

'I'm a big boy, Uncle.'

'And ugly,' his uncle teased, lightening up a little as he reminded Kristof of the running gag between them that had existed since Kris was an annoying youth and his uncle a patient mentor. 'Don't forget ugly.'

'I won't,' Kris promised. 'You wanted an heir for Kaimos Shipping and I delivered,' he said, matching his uncle's upbeat tone. 'See you later. I'll be interested to hear what you think.'

Kimmie stepped away from the door. Shattered. Shocked. Disillusioned. She hadn't meant to eavesdrop. She'd been on the point of joining Kris in the breakfast room, where the friendly housekeeper had told Kimmie she'd find him, and had been a more than unwilling audience to his conversation. But what had been heard could not be unheard, and now she felt betrayed and stupid. He hadn't brought her here to make love, or to discuss the future of their child; that appeared to be already decided—by him and his uncle. She was just a brood mare. She'd done her job, and now she'd do as she was told. Or so he clearly thought.

Her throat dried as she sat down at the foot of the stairs. Her heart was in pieces and her trust in Kris was shattered. The past couldn't be rewound, or she'd wish herself anywhere but here. What to do now? She couldn't just sit here like a lemon, waiting to see what happened next. Nor could she creep away when they had a child to discuss. She had to stand tall and get on with it, but what sort of man got a woman pregnant to satisfy a whim of his uncle, and then compounded the crime by asking that woman to marry him? And now she was going to be looked over like a cow in a country fair?

Choices: she could stay and brazen it out, or she could confront Kris first and then leave. She wasn't the type to run away, so she didn't have an option. These two men were the other half of her baby's family, so she had to tough out the meeting with Kris's uncle, and then confront Kris afterwards. Sucking in a deep, steadying breath, she stood up, crossed the hall, opened the door and walked in.

'Good morning,' Kris said brightly, as if there were no clouds on the horizon and only a reason to feel optimistic about another sunny winter's day. 'I trust you slept well.'

'I trust you did too,' she said mildly, ignoring the laughter dancing in his eyes and the wicked curve of his mouth. Kris had indeed every reason to feel pleased about the way things had turned out.

'I'm going to take you to meet my uncle today. He said he'd like to meet the artist. I bought a few of your paintings—'

'Mandy told me,' she said curtly as she went through the welcome formalities of unfolding a crisp linen napkin and placing it across her lap. 'Just some toast, please,' she told the hovering attendant.

'Certainly, Ms Lancaster. And fresh mint tea, I believe?'

'Correct. Thank you.' How the other half lived. She'd never fit in here.

But Kris's potent charm was such that she couldn't stare unseeing at the table for ever. Nor could she keep the hurt out of her eyes when she looked at him.

'Are you okay?' he asked, picking up on her mood immediately. 'You're not feeling unwell, are you? I've got a very good doctor in London, if you need one.'

'No. Thank you.' She had to look down to escape his penetrating stare. Heartsick. Head sick. Doubting her judgement when it came to men? All of the above, but nothing she was prepared to share with Kris until she'd met his uncle to see what kind of people these men were. 'I just slept too heavily,' she dismissed with a flick of her wrist.

'And woke up grouchy.'

'Not at all.'

'That's good to hear,' he said slowly, seeming a little irked and unconvinced. And no wonder after the amazing night of passion they'd shared. He had to be wondering if she'd faked it and, ironically, if she was the one with something to hide.

'When are we going to meet your uncle?' Suddenly she was in a rush to get this over with—to get everything out in the open, so she could tell them what she thought of them both.

'I thought after breakfast, if that's okay with you?'

There'd be no more passion. Neither of them had

to say a word about that. The mood between them had changed completely. They both knew that today would be a very different day, a serious day when serious matters would be discussed. But first the meeting with Kris's uncle.

'Just be you,' he said when she sat fretting.

Putting his coffee cup down, Kris gave her a long, level stare. 'If you're having second thoughts—'

'About meeting your uncle? I'm not. I'm looking forward to it.'

'You could sound a little more enthusiastic,' he remarked before he asked for more coffee.

'I'm really looking forward to it,' she gritted out. If she had them both in one room she could wipe the floor with them, and then leave with her head held high.

And the baby?

Forget hurt and pain. Most of all, forget anger. She had to listen to what they had to say. Her unborn child was infinitely more important than her pride. She would just have to be as wily as Kris and his uncle as she attempted to, as they would no doubt put it, cut the best deal for her baby.

Cut the best deal?

She felt sick and faint inside.

'Drink some more water,' Kris prescribed as she put a hand to her suddenly clammy forehead.

She drank the glassful down gratefully, and then refused a top-up. 'I feel much better now, but thank you. I'll go and get ready,' she said, turning to face a concerned-looking Kris. Pinning the best smile she could to her trembling mouth, she excused herself from the table, and left the room.

Kris's uncle lived in the most glorious mansion overlooking Regent's Park. Kris had driven them there in the SUV and a man in a smart black suit, seemingly anticipating their arrival, came out of the house and took charge of the vehicle. Opulence embraced her like a scented cashmere throw as a butler swung the double doors wide and she stepped into a very different world indeed. More structured and traditional than Kris's luxurious town house, this was old money—and lots of it.

'I need a minute,' she told Kris, feeling suddenly overwhelmed at the prospect of taking on not just one but two powerful men, and on their own territory, which was so utterly alien to her.

'Of course. I'll wait for you here,' Kris reassured her as the butler ushered Kimmie across the marble-tiled hallway.

This was going so badly wrong, she thought as she leaned for support on the glorious maple surround of a cast concrete sink that was clearly a work of art in its own right. Lifting her chin, she stared at herself in the mirror. She couldn't stay in here all day. So the situation was new. And the surroundings were new to her also, but her inner core of steel remained the same and that was steadfast in its resolve to do the best for her child, always.

'Better?' Kris enquired as she joined him.

'Much better,' she said lightly.

'Then I'll take you to meet my uncle.'

Another surprise awaited her. Far from the fiend who'd urged his nephew to seek out a brood mare, Theo Kaimos turned out to be a charming and amusing man. It didn't take long for her to be completely won over, albeit unwillingly. How had that happened, when she had come here expecting a fight?

'You remind me of my late wife,' he said, holding up a photograph. 'She was a little quirky too, but she made me the happiest man on earth, and we were married for almost forty years. It was a great love affair. Possibly the greatest.'

'She was very beautiful,' Kimmie commented as she stared into the eyes of a woman who seemed calm and happy, and maybe a little bit of a dreamer, as she was.

'The most beautiful,' Theo Kaimos assured her as she handed the photograph back, as only a man who had adored his wife could say with such passion. 'I'm so pleased you came to see me,' he added. 'It's been a long time since I've met someone like you.'

The emotion of that statement hung in the air between them, moving Kimmie almost to tears. Far from disliking Kris's uncle, she could feel his loneliness as if it were her own. She didn't even notice when Kris quietly left the room.

'Stay with me for a while,' Theo urged hopefully. 'You make me feel young again, and I want to hear what you have to say.'

This proved easier than Kimmie could possibly have imagined, and soon the truth was coming out unabridged—all her hopes and fears for the baby, and for herself, and even her feelings for Kris. She'd had no one else to confide in for far too long.

'I just don't know yet,' she admitted honestly. 'I don't know what to think. I overheard his conversation with you on the phone.'

'Listeners never hear good of themselves,' Kris's uncle told her with a rueful smile on his face. 'And are you sure that what you heard was everything? To my mind, you could only have overheard one side of the conversation. Won't you give him another chance?'

'Because of the baby?'

'Why not? Is it so wrong to want the father to take a full part in your child's life?'

'If he does…if he's here…if he can spare the time.'

'Compromises have to be made. That's what a long-term relationship is, Kimmie—a series of compromises and endless consideration for your partner.'

'And our child,' she said.

'And your child,' Theo Kaimos agreed. 'You're lucky…luckier than you know.'

As he spoke, he glanced at the photograph of his late wife, and it put everything in perspective. Kimmie had the power to make choices but, where love and companionship was concerned, Theo Kaimos had none. And so she sat beside him and they talked and talked. Whatever else happened, Kimmie felt as if she'd made a new friend in London. Now it was time to put emotion aside and ask the questions she was longing to ask.

'An heir to the Kaimos Shipping line must be

something you're pleased about,' she suggested, but Theo looked her straight in the eye.

'I won't lie to you; an heir to the shipping line is very welcome,' he confirmed, 'but a grandchild to love and cherish? Now there's the true gift. Kris always considered me his father, and in my heart he is my son, so I hope you won't object to my referring to your child as my grandchild, even though technically I would be a great-uncle?'

'I think you'll be a wonderful grandfather,' Kimmie said honestly.

'All I've ever wanted is for Kristof to be happy,' Theo Kaimos revealed. 'And now I think he has a chance to be, and that's all thanks to you. I can see why Kristof wants to marry you,' he added with a smile.

'Because of this?' She stroked her bump.

'No, because of you,' Kris's uncle stated firmly. 'I like you, Kimmie Lancaster, and, whatever happens between you and Kristof, I want you to promise to come and see me again. Will you do that?'

She stared into misty old eyes that had seen so much of life and love and loss. 'I will,' she whispered. 'I promise.'

Was it possible that Kris might love her? Kimmie wondered as they drove back to his place in the SUV. He had a strange way of showing it, if that were so. She didn't know what to think about the phone conversation she'd overheard but, having met Kris's uncle, she was inclined to give them both the benefit of the doubt. Yes, Theo Kaimos wanted the

Kaimos dynasty to continue, and she couldn't blame him for that—he had no surviving family except for Kris. Had Kris contrived to get her pregnant? Well, if he had, she'd hardly been an unwilling partner. Kris's motives going forward were what mattered. His uncle had assured Kimmie that the baby would have everything it needed, as would she, and she had matched his offer, saying she could manage very well on her own but would hope to see a lot more of him, especially when she had the baby. 'You'll be our child's only grandfather,' she'd pointed out, and they'd hugged. It was a pledge she knew they'd both keep whatever happened between her and Kris.

Kris's commitment when it came to marriage was the only remaining doubt in her mind. Did they need to marry? That was a question for another day. Her feelings for him were too strong to be messed with, and right now she had enough to think about, knowing Theo Kaimos was part of her family. She would never want to exclude him, whatever happened. Nor could she agree to marry Kris for convenience, or for reasons of so-called respectability. Maybe she was a hopeless romantic, but her dream was to cherish, love, adore, and be cherished, loved and adored in return. What she definitely didn't want was an *arrangement*. She wanted to give all her heart, not keep part of it back in case she was hurt again. And she wanted to be loved all the time, not just when it was convenient.

CHAPTER FOURTEEN

'UNCLE THEO LIKES you a lot,' Kris commented.

'And I like your uncle. Very much,' Kimmie confirmed.

'He's been really sick…heart problems, though he's been given the all-clear now, and I've never seen him look better than he did today.'

'News of the baby made him happy.' Kimmie said this without an edge. She was simply stating the truth.

'Yes, it did,' Kris confirmed. 'I think we're all happy.'

'I know I am.'

'Do you doubt me?' he shot back.

'I doubt your motives.'

'Meaning?' Kris frowned.

'Meaning I overheard your phone conversation with your uncle before we left your house. I didn't mean to. I was about to open the door and I couldn't not hear what you said about providing the longed-for heir.'

Heaving a sigh, he sat back as the lights turned red. Forced to stop the car, he turned to face Kimmie. 'Snatches of conversation never tell the whole story.'

'So why do I think this one did?'

'I've no idea.'

'From playboy to devoted father, all within the space of a few months? Does that seem likely to you?'

'Yes, because it's happening. Nothing's set in stone. We make choices and then life throws in some changes and we adapt. When it comes to fathering a child, I adapt like you wouldn't believe.'

'But can you adapt in other ways? I mean, work seems to take up all of your time.'

'I can certainly try,' Kris said with a shrug. 'You're not exactly a slouch yourself,' he pointed out. 'I don't imagine you'll give up painting when you become a mother, will you?'

'I won't be able to afford to.'

'I can make things easier for you.'

'By marrying me?'

'Don't sound so cynical. You might grow to like the idea.'

'Could you compromise enough for that, Kris? I don't see you making allowances for anyone.'

'That's because you don't really know me. You need to spend longer with my uncle,' Kris added dryly.

'Maybe I do,' Kimmie conceded, though she wasn't convinced it would be enough.

Kris had turned into the smart London square where his town house was located. 'What do I have to do to convince you that I'm not as bad as you think I am? This is not just about the Kaimos Shipping line.'

'How do I know that? You must have thought fate had thrown you a lifeline when I pitched up on the beach short of a husband when your uncle had just suggested you look for a wife.'

'Firstly, I follow my own instincts. I love my uncle, but I'm not as susceptible to his charming manipulation as you seem to think. Secondly, you intrigued me, and still do.'

'Really.' Kimmie clenched her jaw. She didn't know what to think. Meeting Kris's uncle had only made things more complicated, because instinctively she trusted him, and he trusted Kris. Passion swirled around them as they stared at each other. Maybe she should climb out of the car and leave this for another day when she was feeling calmer and less confused, but she had never been able to dodge a problem. They hadn't even started to discuss the future of their child, so this stand-off had to end, and it had to end now.

'Is this a set-up? Did you get me pregnant on purpose?' she asked bluntly.

'Haven't I always protected us both?' he countered grimly.

'Yes, but...'

'There are no buts about it. Protection occasionally fails and women get pregnant. You're having my baby, a fact for which I'm eternally glad. There is no set-up here. Yes, there was a moment when, as you said, I thought fate was on my side, but that was because fate had brought me you.' Raking his hair into an even wilder mess, Kris admitted, 'I'm not good with feelings, Kimmie, and even less skilled at expressing them. I learned at a very young age, as did you, to keep my feelings to myself. It became a lifelong habit that I'm finding hard to break, but I do feel something for you...'

'You feel something? What?'

'I honestly don't know. I don't want to overstate it. You're the mother of my child, and I love you for that. You're giving me the family I never had until my uncle took me in, the family he lost when he lost his beloved wife. Of course I love you for that. I'd have to be made of wood not to adore you for what you're giving us.'

'But you can't say anything more to me, personally.'

'Not because I don't feel anything for you,' Kris reiterated tensely, 'but because I don't want to...'

'Raise my hopes?'

'Now you're sounding bitter, and putting words into my mouth. You should know as well as I do that expressing ourselves when it comes to feelings is always guided by the past.'

'I've tried to shake off the past,' Kimmie protested hotly.

'And have you succeeded?' he jeered.

'Have you even tried?' she snapped back.

What she had least wanted happened. The discussion she'd hoped for ended in a row. They bellowed at each other, shouting over each other as words, truths and half-truths—laced with hurt and pain—were glued together with misunderstanding. Neither listened to the other. They fed off the anger in each other's face. Hormones fuelled Kimmie's rage and the tirade grew louder until the windows misted up and even the outside world disappeared, until there were just two people, straining every muscle to rid themselves of the legacy of pain. They beat each other up verbally until there were no words left, and when they finally quieted Kris rested his head back and said, 'I'm done.'

'Me too,' Kimmie agreed numbly.

Reaching for the handle on the passenger door, she climbed out. There was a bus stop at the end of the road and a reliable service that would take her straight home. Kris didn't try to stop her. He didn't leave the car.

'Well,' she murmured to her baby as she walked along the street. 'It's just you and me now. And there won't be any more shouting, ever—I promise. I heard enough of that when I was a little girl, and I'm ashamed of myself. I don't even know where it came from, or how it started. Actually, yes, I do,' she argued with herself. 'I started it. I did everything I've vowed not to do. I allowed everything I've learned to move past to swamp me, to drown me, to threaten me with the possibility of never moving forward. But I won't let it happen again. It's over. It's over for good. Oh, how I wish I hadn't lost my cool... I don't know what happened. I'm normally so calm and, in fairness, so is your daddy...'

'Can I join in this conversation, or is it a conversation just for one?'

Kimmie stopped dead in her tracks. Kris had followed her out of the car. She tensed and turned around. 'You're following me?'

'Making sure you're all right.'

She couldn't blame him for that. She couldn't blame him for anything. Kris had been honourable all along. It was just his commitment to fatherhood that continued to worry her. Would he ever be there for those important occasions that meant so much to a child? Even if it was only a non-speaking role in a Christmas play, it was a precious moment to be cherished, shared and enjoyed. Would he understand that?

'If this is a soliloquy,' he remarked when she remained deep in thought, 'would you rather I left you to it?'

She looked at him, and her heart turned over. The truth was, she'd take him on any terms.

'I'm not stalking you or attempting to control you. I'm just worried about you and want to take care of you,' he said simply.

'That's just it,' Kimmie protested. 'I don't need *looking after.*'

'Everyone needs someone to care for them...even me.'

'Even you?'

'You don't have to believe me,' Kris argued, 'but

I was turning London upside down looking for you before I even knew you were pregnant. I wanted to see you again. I had to see you again.'

'Because?'

'Because you intrigued me.'

Kimmie shook her head with a sad smile on her face. 'Is that your way of saying you like me?'

'I don't know what it is, but it's the truth,' Kris admitted. 'I know work takes up most of my time but, even when I was cutting deals after I'd met you, I kept thinking about you. You're too big a distraction, and one I've discovered I can't function without. I need to get to know you better, so will you please get back in the car?'

'You're so romantic.'

'That's just it—I'm not, but maybe I can learn to be.'

Her bus was coming down the road. It was decision time.

There was no decision to be made, Kimmie realised. Two emotionally stunted people were going to have a child and, one way or another, they had to sort this out so they didn't pass on their sorry heritage to a new, unsuspecting and very vulnerable life, a baby that had done nothing to deserve the fallout from its parents' pasts.

The winter sun was shining brightly as they turned to walk back to the car. There was a beautiful London park across the road and Kris surprised her by suggesting they walk through it. 'Fresh air and space is what we need,' he said. 'I don't feel like being cooped up in a car.'

Neither did Kimmie, and so they entered the park and walked until they found a bench beneath a sheltering copse of trees. For a while neither of them spoke. It was easy to remain silent, lost in their own thoughts while water trickled soothingly into a pond in front of them. It was impossible not to picture bringing their child here to cycle along the paths, or play on the grass in the summertime. Maybe they'd have more than one baby, Kimmie mused. Kris would watch over them while she sketched the scene. As she was doing now, painting a picture of how she would like things to be. But it would never happen. How could it, when Kris didn't have any feelings beyond those of a duty of care, which was amazing, but not enough. She embraced the bump as she thought about it, wanting nothing more than to share the love she felt for the tiny life inside her.

'I know you find it difficult, and maybe impossible, to express your feelings,' she said at last, 'but I'm going to take a chance.' When he turned with a questioning look on his face, she added steadily, 'I love you. I know that sounds crazy after so short a time, but it's true. I love you. You don't have to say anything, but I just wanted you to know how I feel.'

His stomach clenched as though it had received a blow. Kimmie had never been short of courage. He only wished he could find something positive to say in response, but banishing the habit of a lifetime wasn't easy. Expressing how he felt inside did not come naturally and, where Kimmie was concerned, he was in turmoil. There were too many feelings jostling for attention when he was used to feeling nothing.

'We don't have to get married to raise a child successfully,' he said finally, knowing he was being cowardly in not dealing with her statement, but not knowing what else to say. 'My parents were married, and so were yours, and look where that got them.'

'Your uncle was married,' she parried with an understanding look, 'and it seems to have worked out really well for him.'

'So now you want to get married? I'm confused.'

'I didn't say that. I'm just pointing out that different things work for different people.'

'You could live completely independently, if that's what you want, though, selfishly, I hope you don't take that route. Whatever happens, I'll make a financial settlement on our child and, of course, an allowance going forward. As much as you need,' Kris stressed. 'We'll discuss everything going forward, regarding our baby's future, before any decisions are made.'

'So me and the baby don't have to live with you?'

'That's right,' Kris confirmed. 'You can choose any one of my houses or, if you prefer, buy one of your own. You can stay where you are, if that's what you really want to do, but from what I've heard—'

'From Mandy?' Kimmie queried.

'From your good friend,' Kris reminded her.

'There wouldn't be a lot of room there for you and a child, and certainly no garden for our baby to play in when they can walk. But there are other things I want you to know about me before you make up your mind what to do.'

'Such as?' Kimmie waited tensely for Kris to speak.

'You know I'm single-minded about my duty to Kaimos Shipping. Some people would think I'm obsessed to a dangerous degree.'

'But they don't know about your past—' Kimmie leapt in '—or the debt you owe your uncle.'

Kris smiled at her understanding, and it was a relief to see him relax slightly.

'I'm also blinkered and unaware of anything around me when I'm working on a canvas, so I do understand,' she reassured him.

'I've had no reason to act differently until my uncle begged me to stop and think about the future.'

'The future of Kaimos Shipping?'

Kris nodded. 'I thought so at the time, but now I believe he was more concerned about me. He knows all about loneliness and how it can consume you. You made such a difference to him today. Thank you.'

'You don't need to thank me. I enjoyed your uncle's company as much as he seemed to enjoy mine, and I'm looking forward to seeing him again, whatever happens between us. He loves you very much, I do know that, and refers to you as his son. Our child will be his grandchild. I've promised him that.'

'You're a good woman. Is it any surprise that I want you to be my wife?'

'Well, yes, it is, actually. You don't seem to realise that the gulf between us is simply too wide.'

'What do you mean?'

'I mean that I won't come to you as an impoverished painter. My career is by no means certain. And I won't marry someone who, by their own confession, isn't even sure what love is.'

'You can teach me,' he said quietly.

'I could try, but I can't take the risk that I might fail when there's a baby in the middle of our relationship. I think it's better to remain apart, but to come together for anything that concerns our child.'

'It's lonely in our ivory towers,' Kris commented with an ironic huff. 'I don't think either of us can be happy with the sort of relationship you propose.'

'Losing myself in painting has been my salvation, as devoting yourself to your business has been yours. Why change the status quo when we have found a successful formula?'

'A formula,' Kris remarked, unconvinced. 'Can't we try for something more?'

'I'm not sure. Can we?'

They sat in silence for quite a while. It wasn't a tense or angry silence—it was a thoughtful silence.

'What do you want from me, Kimmie?' Kris said at last.

'I want too much,' she admitted. 'I want someone to share everything with, someone who loves me for myself and who won't try to change me. I want a man I can respect and trust, who will protect me when I'm not able to protect myself.'

'I can't imagine that time coming,' Kris admitted, lightening up a little.

'It will when I have a child,' Kimmie admitted. 'I won't be a warrior woman then. I'll be vulnerable. I'll trust the nurses, of course I will, but having someone close, someone special to share that unique moment of happiness with…' Her voice tailed off. 'What will I do if you're away on business when I go into labour? You see my problem,' she said when Kris looked taken aback.

'So marriage is out?'

'It would never work,' Kimmie said confidently. 'I'd stand up to you.'

'And you think I don't want that?'

'I know you don't. You want the easy life, the woman waiting for you with her hair combed and her make-up on, and the children fed, bathed and asleep when you get home from work.'

He laughed out loud, shattering the tension between them into countless tiny shards. 'You're so wrong,' he said, dragging her into his arms. 'Marry me, and I'll take care of you and you'll never feel vulnerable again.'

'I'll just feel lonely when you're not there,' she remarked sadly.

Holding her at arm's length, Kris stared deep into her eyes. He was so easy to succumb to, with those satanic brows and molten black eyes, but she hadn't yet found a way to jump over that gulf between them and until they found a way to bridge it there wasn't a chance she'd accept Kris's proposal.

'I want you,' he ground out.

'I want you too,' she admitted.

'Then marry me.'

'Without love?'

'I didn't say that. You're jumping to conclusions again.'

'Based on everything you've said. Look, I understand a man as rich as you might attract the wrong type of people, but is that a good enough reason to hold your feelings in when you find something you seem to feel so strongly is right? Until you change… that's if you're even capable of changing… I'm not going to agree to marry you. I don't want to fill a vacancy on your staff. I want to be loved wildly and passionately, deeply, and for ever, as your uncle loved your aunt.'

'I'm a realist, not a romantic.'

'Well, when you become a lover, let me know.'

Pulling his head back, Kris stared into her face. 'You're a hard woman, Kimmie Lancaster.'

'I'm anything but,' Kimmie insisted. 'I'm full of love.' As she spoke she stroked her precious bulge. 'And I'm still full of hope for the future, and I want you to be happy too.'

'I will be happy if you agree to marry me.'

'Which amounts to nothing more than signing a piece of paper, just another contract as far as you are concerned. You'll have to try harder than that.'

'Then tell me what to do,' he said, frustrated.

'Express your feelings freely, passionately—don't hold them in a place so deep that even you can't find them. Take a chance, as I did.'

A stiff breeze chose that moment to ruffle Kimmie's hair. Smoothing it back from her face, she turned her collar up. 'Do you think we could go back to the car? It's getting cold out here.'

'Yes, of course,' Kris agreed immediately. 'Let's do that.'

CHAPTER FIFTEEN

THERE WAS ONE area in their lives that neither of them had any trouble in expressing. Physical reassurance could be as potent as countless words, and their needs were mutually pressing. They started off walking at a normal speed down the path, but their footsteps gradually quickened until, reaching for each other's hand, they began to run through the park. Arriving at the car, they dived in and sat tensely while Kris turned on the engine and manoeuvred the growling vehicle through the sluggish London traffic.

'To hell with this!' he exclaimed, swinging the wheel as they approached a private underground car park.

Shadows enveloped them as he drove around and found a space tucked away in a private corner. Parking up, he switched off the engine and then performed some cunning adjustment that made Kimmie's seat fall flat. Moving across the seat, he came to kneel between her legs. Freeing himself, he removed her underwear. 'Yes?'

'Yes!'

'I couldn't wait,' he explained in a throaty husk as he took her deep and began to move.

'So glad…' Kimmie managed to gasp out as she wriggled beneath him to allow an even deeper thrust. '*Ah*, *good…so good*. I'll never get enough of this.'

'It's to be hoped not,' Kris groaned.

It was quite a long time later that they finally sat back and straightened their clothes. It was sexier leaving her with her thoughts and well-used body than talking, Kimmie mused contentedly as Kris flashed his card at the barrier and they drove away.

'Promise me you'll always be spontaneous,' she murmured, leaning back and closing her eyes as he drove smoothly on.

'That's one thing I can promise to do,' he said dryly.

When they pulled up outside his town house, Kris came round to the passenger side. 'My legs are still weak,' she murmured as he helped her down.

'Then I'll carry you.'

'No, that's really not necessary.'

'Yes, it is, Ms Independence,' he assured her as he swung her into his arms and jogged up the steps.

'Put me down and I'll walk,' she protested as Kris opened the door.

'I prescribe rest…eventually,' he amended as the door closed behind them.

'What do you…? Oh,' Kimmie exclaimed softly as Kris stopped halfway up the stairs.

Lowering her carefully on to the plushly carpeted step, Kris freed himself and took her again. This was one time she was glad to have left her underwear off, Kimmie thought, laughing out loud as Kris explained in a matter-of-fact tone, 'I get really good purchase in this position.'

She wasn't about to argue with that. She wasn't about to speak at all. Sometimes actions spoke louder than words and this was one of those times.

'You see,' he said when they paused for breath, 'we don't need to get married to be together.'

'We can just make love on the stairs.'

'As often as we can,' he confirmed, 'though it may get harder as you get more pregnant.'

'I'm sure you'll find a way.'

'So am I,' he said, smiling as he helped her up. 'And, by the way, I've got something for you.'

'Something else?'

'This is serious,' he told her as he carried her the rest of the way up the stairs. 'It's something my uncle wants you to have.'

Shouldering the door to his bedroom, Kris had stripped off her remaining clothes before they even reached the bed. Resting her carefully on the crisply dressed mattress, he stripped off too.

'I thought you had something to give me,' she reminded him.

'I do,' Kris assured her as he began to tease her with just the firm, smooth tip of his formidable erection. 'I have quite a lot to give you.'

Nudging her back onto the firm, supporting pillows, he hooked her legs over his shoulders, spread her wide and took her deep.

That night she slept in Kris's arms, and in the morning they made love again. No words were necessary. They came together by mutual consent and worked effortlessly towards pleasure with the certainty of knowing what each other liked. She dozed afterwards and woke to find Kris fresh from the shower with a white towel wrapped around his washboard waist, looking like that hero from Greek legend again.

'Do you want your present now?'

'I thought I'd just had it,' she murmured groggily, turning over lazily in bed.

'Something more tangible…'

'Than this?' she teased as she caressed her belly. 'You've already given me the only gift I want.'

'But my uncle would like to give you something more…something very special and very dear to him.'

'What is it?' Sitting up in bed, she covered herself with a sheet and waited.

Kris produced a ring box from the nightstand. 'I know you don't like rings unless they come out of a cracker, but I thought you might make an exception in this case.'

'Oh, Kris…' Kimmie's emotions welled as never before as she stared at the beautiful ring.

'I believe my aunt was a little like you, in that she was always impressing on my uncle that it was him she loved and not his money, and so he had this jewel specially set. It's modest, as you can see, but unique and very beautiful.'

That was putting it mildly, Kimmie thought as she reverently removed the ring from its deep blue velvet nest. 'What is the stone?'

'It's a cabochon star sapphire the same colour as my aunt's eyes, with the same light I see in yours. We both thought it would be…appropriate.'

'But how can your uncle bear to part with it?'

Kris hesitated and then shrugged. 'He thought it might help my cause.'

'Your *cause*?'

'When I ask you to marry me,' he said as if this were obvious.

Kris's tone of voice might have been the same to discuss the arrangements for a new office block, Kimmie thought as her heart squeezed tight.

'Kris, we've already been through this,' she said as she carefully put the ring back in the box. Snapping the case shut, she handed it back to him. 'I can't marry someone who doesn't love me, especially when the financial gulf between us is so wide. I would rather continue as I am—'

'Poor but proud?'

'If you like. I'm sorry if I misled you in any way, and please believe me when I say I would do anything not to offend your uncle. This gesture by him is huge and amazing, and generous beyond belief, but I can't accept this ring. And wasn't it you who said we didn't have to get married?'

'We don't,' Kris confirmed, bristling. 'But I thought—'

'For the sake of our child?' Kimmie interrupted. 'Or for the sake of Kaimos Shipping?'

'Well, I hope you know the answer to that by now,' he said tersely. Turning, he pulled on his jeans as if to signify the end of the discussion.

And it had not ended well. Again.

Kimmie set out on foot to walk from Kris's house in an exclusive part of London to the city and her bank. It was time to pick up the reins of her life and she needed some cash. A new start, a new outlook on life—she felt optimistic, not defeated, and, in fairness, Kris had helped with that, by making her feel beautiful, wanted, desired for the first time in her life.

But even he had an angle: an heir for Kaimos Shipping. Her love for him was as simple and as complicated as that. Yes, they would share responsibility for their child and split the time between them, they had decided. Lots of families did that successfully, and it was wrong to want more, she had insisted. But she did want more. She wanted the family she'd never had, but perhaps that was as much a fantasy as the dreams she depicted in her paintings. Even so, she remained positive as she hurried along, smiling to herself. It wasn't everyone who said, *No, thank you,* to a billionaire's proposal. Yes, but wasn't that a hollow triumph? Kimmie mused as she entered the bank. She loved Kris. She would always love Kris, no matter what the future held for them.

For some reason her card wouldn't work in the cash machine. The queues were long in front of the counter, so she asked to see the manager. She didn't have to wait long before she was called into the office.

'What do you mean there's no money in my personal account?' she demanded. 'I know I instructed you to close my business account, but…'

'Your accounts were still linked,' the manager explained stiffly, 'and so the money in your personal account went to paying off the significant overdraft in your business account before we then closed it. It's the bank's policy.'

What a mess. So much for pride. The bank manager had warned her before that Mike had emptied the business account—he'd clearly done more than that. She should have checked her balances, but life had been so hectic recently. Now all she wanted was to leave the manager's office before the stifling air of condescension smothered her.

'Thank you,' she said. *For nothing*, she thought, holding her head up high as she left the room.

It was raining when she reached the street. Of course it was. How fitting. She had a baby to think about and no money at all. Finally forced to a halt by pedestrian lights that, obviously, were also against her, she had the humiliating task of checking the few coins in her purse before deciding if she could afford to duck inside a roadside café to shelter herself from the rain.

'Flat decaf and a packet of caramel wafers, please,' she said when it was her turn in the queue. Both came under the heading of emergency rations, and could therefore be justified. She had two pounds twenty pence exactly left in her purse, which wasn't even enough for her bus fare home. As she waited, she noticed a sign. Reading was a distraction, and she had something of a history with signs. This one read Staff Needed.

'Can I help you?' the young woman behind the counter asked, seeing Kimmie's interest.

The barista looked nice and friendly and so Kimmie dived straight in. 'I need a job and you're advertising for staff?'

'Do you have any experience?'

'Well, yes, but no, I mean…'

'Which is it?'

This was not her finest moment. Still reeling from the news at the bank, she had tears in her eyes. 'I know how to make coffee,' she offered lamely.

The barista smiled sympathetically. 'I'm really sorry. We should have taken that notice down. The position has been filled. No. Really, it has,' the barista insisted. 'Why don't you try further down the high street? There are always flyers on the shop windows advertising jobs down there.'

For out of work artists whose only experience was with a paintbrush?

'Thank you. I will,' Kimmie said as she went to find a seat. Predictably, every seat was taken.

For someone who'd been self-supporting for as long as she had, this new development took some getting used to. She thought about Kris. If the gulf between them had been unbridgeable before, what was it now?

She couldn't tell anyone. Why burden them with her stupidity? With nothing else to do, she checked her phone. There was a message from Mandy to let her know that people were already asking about Kimmie's next exhibition, and a text from Kris that made her heart pound: *Are you okay? Let me know.* She couldn't fault him for his sense of duty and caring nature. If only he could express his emotions as freely... *I'm fine*, she replied. Adding a kiss seemed inappropriate. Theirs was more of a business relationship now. There was also a lovely little message from Kyria Demetriou that made her eyes sting, and made her long for things that seemed permanently out of reach, like a simple life where people loved each other openly, and where everyone was kind and smiled a lot. It was time to start painting again, she concluded.

And she would buy paint and canvas how, exactly?

'To what do I owe this honour?'

Kris flinched inwardly as Kimmie silently, but quite obviously, braced herself, before saying whatever it was she had come to say.

'You don't mind?' she said, glancing around, her cheeks flushed with embarrassment. 'I mean, my coming here to your office in town?'

'Of course I don't.' With a look at his PA, he indicated his wish not to be interrupted until further notice. His agenda was full for the day, but never too full to accommodate Kimmie. 'What can I do for you?' he said as soon as the door had closed. 'Sit down,' he invited, choosing a chair where she could look over the landmarks of London without feeling she must stare straight at him. 'Would you like something to drink?'

'I just had a drink down the road, thank you.'

'Then stop wringing your hands and tell me what's on your mind. Come on, Kimmie. This isn't like you. You always come straight out with things. Where's my Warrior Woman gone?'

'She's on a break,' Kimmie admitted dryly, but it was a poor attempt at humour and her shoulders slumped. As he might have expected, her dejection didn't last long and, lifting her chin, she informed him, 'The woman you see before you now is Crushed Woman... Broke Woman... Woman in Need of a Loan.'

'Well, if that's all...'

The look she gave him reminded him they were both survivors. 'I've never asked you for money and I'm not going to start now,' she said.

'Tell me what's happened, though I should tell you that I can't see you as Crushed Woman. You're more of a cork than a piece of tinfoil.'

'How flattering.'

But she was smiling. 'I try my best,' he said, straight-faced. 'So, how can I help you to bob up again this time?'

'I need a loan to buy canvas and paint, but I'll pay you back.'

'You need a loan?' he echoed, frowning.

CHAPTER SIXTEEN

'WHAT'S HAPPENED TO US, Kimmie?'

'What do you mean, "What's happened to us?"'

'You accuse me of never showing my feelings, but do you always show yours? Saying the words "I love you" is far easier than testing that love, isn't it? I know,' he added before she had a chance to reply. 'I haven't even gone as far as saying the words. I haven't, because I didn't want to lead you on, and I just couldn't be sure that what I was feeling wasn't a weird sort of triumph—not connected with providing an heir for Kaimos Shipping, but becoming a father. Knowing that, if all went well, I would become a parent, and could show my child the love my parents weren't able to offer me, was immense. I was overwhelmed by it and, after a lifetime of suppressing my feelings, it took some getting used to.'

'And now?' she asked tremulously.

'And now you come to ask me for a loan, and tell me you're fine, when clearly that's not the case. Who's hiding their feelings now, Kimmie?'

When she didn't speak, he added, 'I can only

imagine what it cost you to come here.' The fact
that she had nowhere else to go didn't lessen the im-
pact of a proud, self-sufficient woman like Kimmie
throwing herself on his mercy.

'It wasn't easy,' she admitted ruefully, 'but if I
don't paint I don't make money, and I need to start
earning right away. To do that I have to buy sup-
plies.' Her lips pressed down in a sad little smile as
she shrugged. 'Will you lend me the money? I'll pay
you back every penny. You do trust me to do that,
don't you?'

'I trust you with my life, and with the life of our
child. You can have anything. You know that.'

Trust was everything to Kimmie. It was the rock
she had always wanted to build her life on, but that
rock had so often turned out to be sand.

And, much as he wanted to gift her the money, a
handout wasn't the answer. She wouldn't want one.
Kimmie had come to him because she needed to
get back on her feet and for no other reason, unfortunately.

'I'll organise a transfer.'

'Thank you,' she whispered.

'And set out the terms of the loan.'

She raised her head at that and when she said,
'Thank you,' this time her voice was firm and her
eyeline was steady. 'I'd appreciate that.'

'I knew you would,' he said, mouth tugging up at
one corner in a smile. 'Truce?'

'Truce,' she agreed. 'And thank you again...for
understanding.'

'Of course I understand. You're a success-ful woman who's had a few bumps along the way. Haven't we all? You'll move past it. Life's like that. And with the benefit of hindsight you might see that all this has happened for a reason.'

'What reason?' Squeezing her eyes tightly shut, she grimaced. 'And does it have to hurt quite so much?'

'Rejoice that you're feeling something. It's been a long time…for both of us and, yes, as I said before, it takes some getting used to. I'll make sure the transfer is in your bank right away. I'll mail the details of the repayment plan. And now, if that's all…?'

'Oh, yes… I'm sorry. I realise this is a working day. I shouldn't take up any more of your time.'

And now he felt bad. She looked stricken as she made for the door. He got there before her and barred her way. 'Kimmie…'

'Goodbye, Kris. I won't forget your kindness.'

'You'd better not,' he warned, standing aside so she could leave. 'Or our baby will have a rocky start to family life, and I don't think either of us wants that, do we?'

Her eyes filled with tears. 'No,' she whispered, 'that's the last thing we want.'

It was as though her tears had finally broken through a barrier inside him. He had meetings that couldn't be cancelled. Board meetings could be post-poned, site visits rescheduled, team meetings de-layed… Ambassadors offering huge contracts? Not so much.

He cancelled anyway.

'You're right,' he called out, catching up with Kimmie as she was about to cross the road in front of Kaimos Shipping's gleaming steel and glass totem to excellence.

'Sorry?' She whirled around.

'You're right about me and business,' he explained. 'There are more important things in life.'

'Like what?' she queried, frowning.

'Like my love for you.'

'What?'

He ushered her back into the building. Calling his driver, he arranged for the limo to take them home.

All the way back he held Kimmie in his arms. There was no need to speak. They'd said everything. Now it was time to turn those words into actions.

'Why did I get myself into such a mess?' she asked, not expecting an answer, he guessed, as they entered the house.

'Do you think I've never blundered? You learn by your mistakes,' he said, guiding her into the library, his favourite room in the house. 'It's part of the game in business.'

'But this isn't a game,' she whispered. 'This is my heart.'

'And you feel as if it's been trampled on so many times there's no point in trying to revive it? Come on, Kimmie, I know you better than that. We've both come a long way since we met on that beach,' he added as he ushered her towards a comfortable sofa in front of the log fire. 'I've not quite perfected the art of being romantic, but I'm working on it.'

'By drawing up another contract?'

'Yeah. That's what you wanted, isn't it?'

'Absolutely,' she confirmed, but there was tension in her voice.

'I'm still open to offers to repay the loan in kind.'

'I bet you are,' she said, loosening up as she gazed at him.

'And yes, people are supposed to be nice to each other, but that doesn't always happen.' He shrugged. 'We both know that. We're not children cowering in a corner as we used to, waiting to see how things turn out. We make things happen now.'

'Is that what you're doing?'

He ignored the question. 'You know how to grab hold of life and ride that wave,' he insisted. 'And you'll do so again, though next time I predict you'll take more of an interest in the business side of your career.'

'I might need some help with that.'

'I'm offering. Drink?'

'How can you turn in a flash from an offer that has to be priceless in the world of commerce to something as mundane as a drink?'

'Try this for a switch-around.' Getting down on one knee on the rug in front of the fire, he brought out a ring box, for the third time and hopefully final time, although he knew he'd ask her as many times as it took to get the answer he wanted. 'I think you know what I'm going to ask, but I'm going to ask it anyway. Kimmie Lancaster, I love you with all my heart, and I promise never to stop you doing anything you want to do, and that includes borrowing money from me—though if I don't get the right answer this time I might decide to charge interest on the loan.'

'Retrospectively?'

'Whatever it takes.'

'I don't know what to say.'

'How about yes?'

'Seriously?' Slipping down onto the floor in front of him, Kimmie raised her chin. 'Can we do this?' she asked in all seriousness.

'Of course we can. We can do anything we want, so long as we remain true to each other.'

'I don't want your money.'

'Fortunately, that's not what I'm offering.'

'What are you offering?'

'My name, as well as something far more valuable than cash in the bank.'

'Which is?'

'My experience in business. As a successful artist—and, yes, you *are* successful, and are going to be even more so—it's your duty to become familiar with how commerce works. I'm not offering you a handout, or even an easy path. It will be hard work repaying my loan. I'm a relentless taskmaster. You'll pay me back in full, and every penny I receive will go straight into the scholarship fund you're trying to build. That will be your incentive. The fund will be a success and so will you. I believe in you. Now believe in yourself.'

She was quiet for quite a while, and then she mused out loud, 'Mandy said something similar.'

'Then listen to us.'

If Kris had offered pity or an unconditional loan, she would probably have thrown everything back in his face, but she realised he knew her too well for that. And he'd admitted that he loved her. That was a colossal thing for him.

'I love you too,' she said, which was still a colossal thing for Kimmie to say, even though she'd already told him once before. They deserved each other, she concluded as Kris smiled with fierce satisfaction. 'With all my heart.'

'For ever and always,' he confirmed.

And then he kissed her and held her as if he would never let her go. She didn't want to go anywhere. She was home.

The sale of a large canvas of Kyria Demetriou staring out to sea in thoughtful mood paid off Kimmie's loan to Kris, and added a hefty sum to her scholarship programme. There had been a vast increase in demand for her paintings, and this last sale had prompted a new exhibition.

'I've got something for you,' she said.

'You do choose your moments,' Kris remarked, precariously balancing on the top of a ladder to adjust one of her paintings.

'Can I give it to you now?'

'Can't it wait?'

'Maybe, but...I don't know.'

'You infuriating woman,' Kris growled as he sprang down from the ladder.

'Feel this…' Pressing her back into him, Kimmie wrapped Kris's arms around her heavily pregnant belly. 'The baby's turning somersaults. I thought you'd want to feel…'

'I do want to feel.' Brushing her hair aside, he kissed her neck as they stood motionless in wonder.

'Pretty good, huh?' Kimmie commented happily.

'We seem to have got the recipe right,' Kris agreed, smiling.

Turning her, he kissed her tenderly and held her close. 'For ever and always,' he reminded her.

They strolled down the same hall in the same community centre that had become a magnet for those eager to view the works of new artists. 'I hope you can feel my appreciation for your work?' Kris teased as he dragged Kimmie close at the end of the hall.

'I can certainly feel something,' she confirmed. 'Do you have any idea of how sexy you look when you're up a ladder in rugged boots, snug-fitting jeans and a soft wool jumper with the sleeves rolled back to reveal forearms like steel bars?'

Kris pulled a face. 'Honestly? It's never occurred to me.' He laughed. 'You, on the other hand…'

'Not here,' Kimmie protested. 'Anyone could walk in.' The hall was a public place and plenty of people were working on preparation for this latest exhibition.

'Isn't that half the fun?' Kris suggested as he took full advantage of the love of his life.

'For you, maybe,' Kimmie gasped as he upped the risk, making her groan with pleasure. 'Don't you need to be doing something useful with that spirit level?' she asked, glancing wildly at the picture he'd been hanging.

'I *do*,' he agreed. 'I definitely do. Are you complaining?' he asked as she gasped.

'Never!'

EPILOGUE

THE KAIMOS WEDDING was held in the grand salon on board Kristof Kaimos's fabulous superyacht, affectionately nicknamed the *Office Block* by its new joint owner, his beloved.

Everyone agreed the couple were perfectly matched, even though they were so utterly different. Take one hard, driven businessman and one boho artist, mix them together, and the result was a loving family with just the right balance of artistry and commerce to keep love at the top of both their agendas.

No one who saw them with their infant child could deny the love that radiated from them. There had never been a more beautiful bride, people said, even if her hair *was* a little unusual. And as for her husband, the impossibly handsome Kristof Kaimos, billionaire, now a lover and a father, who didn't care if the world knew he was besotted with his wife, and enchanted by their baby daughter, Camilla. His happiness had only seemed to make him more successful in business, and Kaimos Shipping had gone from strength to strength.

Everyone who mattered to the couple joined them on their happy day, and Kimmie was proud to wear the ring that had meant so much to Kris's uncle. Happily, another friendship seemed to be blossoming between Theo Kaimos and Kyria Demetriou and, as far as Kimmie and Kris were concerned, that put the seal on the day.

Kris had never seen anyone lovelier than his bride and knowing Kimmie was quite capable of choosing her own path through life, and yet had chosen to walk that path with him, was something he valued more than he could say…though he did have a good go at saying it, because they'd vowed to be honest with each other always and express their feelings fully.

No one mattered more to Kris than this woman standing at his side and their baby daughter. Who knew he could become such a devoted family man?

'I knew,' his uncle had assured him with vigour. 'I always knew that when the right woman came along you would be smitten. It just took a little longer than I thought for you to realise Kimmie was the one. Me? I knew right away.'

'Of course you did, Uncle.'

But now, as he looked at Kimmie, he knew his uncle was right. He should have been telling her how special she was from the very first moment they'd met instead of fighting falling in love quite so hard. Each day he'd learned more about her, and each day he had more reason to love her than before, and he told her this in every way he could.

The fresh white rose petals he'd had specially imported sent billows of glorious scent wafting around her. The setting was everything he'd hoped for, and that was all thanks to his wonderful staff, under the dedicated supervision of Mandy, ably assisted by Kyria Demetriou.

'I love you,' Kimmie whispered as the ceremony was about to begin.

Quite suddenly it was as if he, Kimmie and their baby daughter, who was safe in Kyria Demetriou's arms, were the only three people present. 'I love you too,' he said, staring deep into Kimmie's eyes, and then the congregation fell silent and the marriage ceremony began.

The love surrounding them was almost like a living thing, Kimmie thought and, yes, she wanted to paint it.

'Stop designing sketches in your mind, and just say "I do",' he advised, staring down in a way that made her body tremble and yearn for his touch.

'I do,' she stated clearly, and then the minister declared them husband and wife.

'So my dress isn't too plain for you?'

'Your dress is perfect.'

'Perfect to take off?'

'That too,' Kris confirmed, smiling into her eyes when they were alone together at last.

She wore the simple ivory silk sheath with fresh flowers in her hair and the beautiful star sapphire ring as her only other adornment. As she'd asked, her wedding ring was a plain gold band.

'I love painting hands and rings that seem to grow into a person's hand as they get older, just as you are part of me,' she'd told Kris.

'I'll never change you,' he said now as her dress pooled on the floor at Kimmie's feet.

'It's too late,' she said. 'You've already changed me.'

'As you have changed me,' he said and, lifting her hands to his lips, Kris kissed each one in turn in a silent pledge of trust and love.

* * * * *

If you enjoyed
The Greek's Virgin Temptation
you're sure to enjoy these other stories
by Susan Stephens!

A Night of Royal Consequences
The Sheikh's Shock Child
Pregnant by the Desert King
A Scandalous Midnight in Madrid

Available now!

#3753 THE SICILIAN'S SURPRISE LOVE-CHILD
One Night With Consequences
by Carol Marinelli

Innocent Aurora is everything tycoon Nico shouldn't want. But even his famous control isn't a match for their combustible chemistry... Then Nico discovers their encounter has left her pregnant! Will Aurora's revelation give this Sicilian a reason to risk *everything*?

#3754 CINDERELLA'S SCANDALOUS SECRET
Secret Heirs of Billionaires
by Melanie Milburne

Isla is carrying famous hotelier Rafe's baby! No one can know—the last thing she wants is to make the headlines. But when Rafe learns about her pregnancy, he's intent on marrying her!

#3755 THE GREEK'S BILLION-DOLLAR BABY
Crazy Rich Greek Weddings
by Clare Connelly

A tragic loss has led outrageously wealthy Leo to deny himself all pleasure. Until he meets innocent Hannah at a party in Greece... That night, Leonidas breaks all his rules, indulging in red-hot oblivion—with inescapable consequences!

#3756 CLAIMING MY BRIDE OF CONVENIENCE
by Kate Hewitt

My terms were clear: money in exchange for her becoming Mrs. Matteo Dias—on paper, at least. But as Daisy, the shy waitress I married, reveals a spirited side, it's high time I claim my convenient bride!

#3757 A PASSIONATE REUNION IN FIJI
Passion in Paradise
by Michelle Smart

Workaholic billionaire Massimo has convinced his estranged wife, Livia, to accompany him to Fiji. Trapped in paradise, an explosive reunion is in the cards, but only if their passion can burn away their past...

#3758 VIRGIN PRINCESS'S MARRIAGE DEBT
by Pippa Roscoe

At a Paris ball, Princess Sofia meets a man she never thought she'd see again—billionaire Theo. Now, as their chemistry reignites, Theo creates a scandal to finally claim Sofia's hand—in marriage!

#3759 THE INNOCENT'S EMERGENCY WEDDING
Conveniently Wed!
by Natalie Anderson

Katie can't believe she's asking notorious playboy Alessandro to marry her! It's only temporary, but when Alessandro tests the boundaries of their arrangement, untouched Katie finds herself awakened to unknown, but oh-so-tempting, desire...

#3760 DEMANDING HIS DESERT QUEEN
Royal Brides for Desert Brothers
by Annie West

Desert prince Karim needs a bride—and Queen Safiyah is the perfect choice. Yet the pain of their broken engagement years ago remains. Karim's demands are simple: a convenient marriage for their country's sake. Except Safiyah still fires his blood...

YOU CAN FIND MORE INFORMATION ON UPCOMING HARLEQUIN® TITLES, FREE EXCERPTS AND MORE AT WWW.HARLEQUIN.COM.

HPCNM0919RB

Get 4 FREE REWARDS!

We'll send you 2 FREE Books
plus 2 FREE Mystery Gifts.

Harlequin Presents® books feature a sensational and sophisticated world of international romance where sinfully tempting heroes ignite passion.

FREE
Value Over
$20

"Hiding away?" Livia asked.

"Taking a breather."

Dark brown eyes studied him, a combination of sympathy and amusement in them. Livia knew well how social situations made him feel.

She caught the barman's attention and ordered herself a bourbon, too. "This is a great party."

"People are enjoying it?"

"Very much." She nudged him with her elbow and pointed at one of the sofas. Two of the small children he'd almost tripped over earlier were fast asleep on it. A third, who'd gone a pale green color, was eating a large scoop of ice cream, utter determination etched on her face. "Someone needs to get that girl a sick bag."

He laughed and was immediately thrown back to his sister's wedding again.

He'd approached Livia at the bar. She'd said something inane that had made him laugh. He wished he could remember what it was but it had slipped away the moment she'd said it, his attention too transfixed on her for words to stick.

She'd blown him away.

Those same feelings…

Had they ever really left him?

The music had slowed in tempo. The dance floor had filled, the children making way for the adults.

"We should dance," he murmured.

Her chest rose, head tilted, teeth grazing over her bottom lip. "I suppose we should…for appearance's sake."

He breathed deeply and slowly held his hand out.

Equally slowly, she stretched hers out to meet his. The pads of her fingers pressed into his palm. Tingles shot through his skin. His fingers closed over them.

On the crowded dance floor, he placed his hands loosely on her hips. Her hands rested lightly on his shoulders. A delicate waft of her perfume filtered through his airwaves.

He clenched his jaw and purposely kept his gaze focused above her head.

They moved slowly in tempo with the music, their bodies a whisper away from touching…

"When did you take your tie off?" Livia murmured when she couldn't take the tension that had sprung between them any longer.

She'd been trying very hard not to breathe. Every inhalation sent Massimo's familiar musky heat and the citrus undertones of his cologne darting into her airwaves. Her skin vibrated with awareness, her senses uncoiling, tiny springs straining toward the man whose hands hardly touched her hips. She could feel the weight in them though, piercing through her skin.

Caramel eyes slowly drifted down to meet her gaze.

The music beating around them reduced to a burr.

The breath of space between them closed. The tips of her breasts brushed against the top of his flat stomach. The weight of his hands increased in pressure.

Heat pulsed deep in her pelvis.

Her hands crept without conscious thought over his shoulder blades. Heart beating hard, her fingers found his neck…her palms pressed against it.

His right hand caressed slowly up her back. She shivered at the darts of sensation rippling through her.

Distantly, she was aware the song they were dancing to had finished.

His left hand drew across her lower back and gradually pulled her so close their bodies became flush.

Her cheek pressed into his shoulder. She could feel the heavy thuds of his heart. They matched the beats of hers.

His mouth pressed into the top of her head. The warmth of his ragged breath whispered in the strands of her hair. Her lungs had stopped functioning. Not a hitch of air went into them.

A finger brushed a lock of her hair.

She closed her eyes.

The lock was caught and wound in his fingers.

She turned her cheek and pressed her mouth to his throat…

A body slammed into them. Words, foreign to her drumming ears but unmistakably words of apology, were gabbled.

They pulled apart.

There was a flash of bewilderment in Massimo's eyes she knew must be mirrored in hers before he blinked it away.

A song famous at parties all around the world was now playing. The floor was packed with bodies all joining in with the accompanying dance. Even the passed-out children had woken up to join in with it.

And she'd been oblivious. They both had.

Don't miss
A Passionate Reunion in Fiji.
Available October 2019 wherever
Harlequin® Presents books and ebooks are sold.

www.Harlequin.com

Want to give in to temptation with
steamy tales of irresistible desire?

Check out **Harlequin® Presents®,
Harlequin® Desire** and
Harlequin® Kimani™ Romance books!

New books available every month!

CONNECT WITH US AT:

Facebook.com/groups/HarlequinConnection

 Facebook.com/HarlequinBooks

 Twitter.com/HarlequinBooks

 Instagram.com/HarlequinBooks

 Pinterest.com/HarlequinBooks

ReaderService.com

**ROMANCE WHEN
YOU NEED IT**

PGENRE2018